MW01136002

Books by Jane O'Brien

The White Pine Trilogy:
The Tangled Roots of Bent Pine Lodge #1
The Dunes & Doll's Antiques Emporium #2
The Kindred Spirit Bed & Breakfast #3

The Lighthouse Trilogy:
The 13th Lighthouse #1
The Painted Duck #2
Owl Creek #3

The Unforgettables:
Ruby and Sal #1
Maisy and Max #2
Ivy and Fox #3

Ivy

and

Fox

Copyright © 2017 by Jane O'Brien All Rights Reserved No part of this publication may be reproduced, stored in a retrieval system, or transmitted by any means – electronically, mechanically, photographic (photocopying), recording, or otherwise – without prior permission in writing by the author. Printed in the United States of America and Published by: Bay Leaf Publishing

Connect with Jane O'Brien

www.authorjaneobrien.com

http://www.amazon.com/author/obrienjane

www.facebook.com/janeobrien/author/

Contact: authorjaneobrien@gmail.com

This book is dedicated to all of those who have gone before me. Whether it be my Ukrainian ancestors, my German ancestors, my Scots/Irish or my English ancestors, I am truly grateful for the sacrifices you made to come to this glorious country where I have been privileged to be born. Even though I have only met a few generations of you, I feel you in my heart; the tug is strong when I visit your graves and read your documents. The connection is real. Without you my stories would not have been written.

There's one sad truth in life I've found

While journeying east and west -

The only folks we really wound

Are those we love the best.

We flatter those we scarcely know,

We please the fleeting guest,

And deal full many a thoughtless blow

To those who love us best.

~Ella Wheeler Wilcox

Table of Contents

Dictionary of Ukrainian and Gypsy Words:

Gypsy – a traveler

Romani or Romany – the preferred name for a gypsy

Tsyhany – Ukrainian for Romani

Gadjo or Gadji – male or female for a non-Romani

Hutsuls and Boykos – ethno-cultural groups of the Ukraine in the Carpathians

Musical Instruments:

Tsymboly – hammered dulcimer

Sopilka – decorated wooden flute like a recorder.

Balalaika – Russian triangular guitar

Bubon – tambourine

Lozhky – decorated wooden spoons

Prologue – Ukraine, 1868

Anya was lying flat on her back, gazing at the sky. The damp grass was beginning to soak through her dress, but she didn't care. She wore many layers of garment, and it would be a while before the dampness reached her skin. This was her favorite time of the day, when the sun dipped below the horizon but left just enough light behind to illuminate her surroundings, which were now colored in a soft blue haze.

The stars were exceptionally clear tonight; she wished she knew more about the constellations. She had been told the stars formed to make pictures and each picture had a name, but without any formal schooling she could only guess at what others saw. She tried to make pictures of her own by imagining lines drawn from one star to another, but all she was able to create were triangles and squares. 'I guess I have not been blessed with any creativity,' she thought.

Sasha snuggled in beside her, but always the working dog, he kept his eyes scanning the flock. His warmth felt good and was a comfort to the young woman who was all alone on the hillside of the Carpathian Mountains. This was the most dangerous time of day for them all. Predators were everywhere; that's why the dog was essential to life. The sheep quietly bleated, calling each other to make sure their lambs were nearby and safe. Sasha turned around a few times and then settled in for a few moments of sleep, knowing that Anya was alert. The dog's job began when the darkness was so black that only a canine could see through it. Once Anya fell asleep, the loyal sheepdog would move quietly among the flock throughout the night to make sure all was well. It was the only way Anya could get any rest. If she returned to the village in the valley herding fewer sheep than she had gone up the mountain with, there would be consequences that she could not bear to think about. Her father was a hard taskmaster, but it was because the sheep were their only livelihood. They were to be protected at all costs.

Anya had been coming up the mountain from her Ukrainian village every summer since she turned thirteen, and nothing horrible had ever happened, but she was warned each time she left that there was always a first time, so she must be alert. Anya would spend one whole month in the grasslands all by herself, with no one but her dog and nothing with which to protect herself but her skinning knife, and a bow and arrow. The first time she came here, when she was ten, she only stayed for one week, but that time she was with her older brother. They came together two more summers after that. He taught her everything she needed to know to care for the flock, but her brother was gone now. He lost his life in a tragic accident when he fell off the hay wagon and broke his neck. The other brothers and sisters had all married; they had their own families to take care of now, so it was up to her to keep the family flock strong and healthy. The way things were going, it looked like she would be responsible for the flock for years to come, and would most likely become an old maid, the only child left to care for Mama and Papa. Anya was already nineteen years old, and so far there were no prospects of marriage to a suitor her own age. It was beginning to be an embarrassment for her parents.

Anya was very beautiful, with an oval face, large blue eyes, and a clear rosy complexion, thanks to the fresh mountain air. Her cheekbones were high and prominent, framed by her sandy brown hair which she always kept neatly braided and wrapped tightly around her head. The problem was her personality. She could be quite judgmental at times, and sharp of tongue. She knew she should try to soften her ideas of a perfect mate, because none of the men or young boys in the village suited her fancy, and she refused to marry until one of them did. The list of eligible men was short, and unless she wanted to marry a cousin or an old man, – which might happen if Papa had anything to say about it – she would end up a spinster. Recently, there had been talk of her marrying Leonid Palyichak, but he was already fifty, with gray hair and a round fat belly. He had plenty of money, a large farm, and a substantial herd of cattle. Papa said it would be a good alliance for the family, but Anya would rather die than consent to that arrangement. Maybe there would be a sign in the stars tonight that would tell her what to do. Papa had promised he would not force her, but she knew if she didn't agree to the marriage, the rest of their lives would be difficult, and she would feel guilty. Times were tough. The Russians, the Austrians, and the Polish all wanted a piece of the lush farmlands of Ukraine. 'Won't they ever leave us alone and in peace?' she thought. 'Don't we deserve our own homeland like everyone else?'

Anya linked her fingers tightly together and began a prayer to God, asking to show her the way. "Please, Father, let my people live in peace. Let my family be rich with food, and help me to make the right decision for my life, for myself, and for Mama and Papa. I will put it all into your hands if you will only show me the way. Please give me a sign if you believe that I should marry Leonid. I will trust in whatever you have in store for me." Anya waited for a full five minutes in silence, all the while with her hands folded together. There was nothing, no sounds at all but a few nightbird calls. Then Anya whispered, "Please, Lord, tell me if you have someone saved for me. Show me that you have my life planned out, and I promise that where you lead, I will follow." At that exact moment a shooting star crossed the heavens. It was so bright, Anya could see the entire field before her. Tears came to her eyes. He had heard her! God had listened to her plea. She kissed her rosary, always so near to her heart, and then made the sign of the cross, saying, "Thank you, Lord. In the name of the Father, the Son, and the Holy Ghost. Amen."

"Did you see that Sasha? We are going to be okay. God has something wonderful planned for us. Something we could never foresee or make happen on our own. I can't wait to find out what it is -- or *who* it is." She clapped her hands together with excitement and then laughed aloud as Sasha licked her face, thumping his tail over Anya's joy.

Present Day

Chapter One

"A penny for your thoughts."

His voice seemed to come from a faraway place. A slow smile spread across her face. She must have been dozing in the morning sun. She felt warm, but not hot. It was more -- she hesitated in her thoughts as she searched for the right word. Comfortable was not correct, but she was. Lazy was also not correct, but she did feel lazy. Perfect -- that was it. She felt perfect -- perfectly contented and perfectly complete. Ivy opened her eyes and looked up at the man who was hers. All hers since last June. She was Mrs. Fox Marzetti, and therefore part of a huge Italian-American family. She rubbed her thumb over the rings on the fourth finger of her left hand. They were still new to her and they sometimes twisted on her finger, not having made that groove that all married couples had after time. When the ring changed position and the large diamond poked her pinky finger, she would glance down and see the gorgeous set which flashed brightly in the lights. She had a family – a real family of her own.

And then there was the little man who had always been hers, from the moment she felt the first kick. He chattered in his baby gibberish, words understood only by him, while he played on the wet beach sand with his shovel and bucket. He loved to throw the wet mud into the lake. It seemed to give him great joy when it made a splash. But usually he couldn't make it that far, his little arms still too weak to throw any distance, so he ended up waddling with a shovelful into the water's edge and dropping the mud there. Ivy knew Fox was keeping a close watch on him. She trusted him with their son one hundred percent.

Realizing she still hadn't answered Fox, she placed her two fingers on her lips and then touched them to his lips. It was something they had started to do when one person was too busy or dirty to plant a real one, as they often were with the many projects around the house that required sweat equity. "If you must know, I was in another world. One of my own creation, of course." She laughed at herself, knowing how foolish that sounded.

"I thought so," he said, the crinkle lines around his eyes showing with his smile. "You do tend to daydream a lot, Mrs. Marzetti."

"I guess it's the plight of a writer. I'm actually stuck for a new storyline. I have writer's block for the first time."

"Why do you need to worry about it? 'Maisy and Max' has skyrocketed, and it's only been out since spring. It's doing amazingly well. Can't you take a break and give yourself time to rejuvenate? There's been a lot going on since our wedding and the book release."

"Yes, I could. My publisher is not asking for anything else, yet. But I guess it's my own inner drive, and besides I'd like to keep the momentum going. It's just that I don't know where to go next. Nothing comes to me at all. I think the Maisy and Max/Ruby and Sal story line is finished. It all ends with me and you, and little Sal of course. Other than a few close friends and relatives, no one knows how true the story really is. If anyone ever found out about the necklace, we could never live in peace again." She grimaced at the thought of their private space being invaded.

"There are a few people who know -- Ronnie, your distant cousin, for one. Without her help we would never have known 'the rest of the story,' as Paul Harvey used to say."

"Who's Paul Harvey?"

Fox laughed. "I'm sure you're too young to know, but he was a famous radio personality who always ended his show with the statement, 'and now you know the rest of the story."

"Interesting. And how do you know that? You're only a few years older than I am. When was the last time you listened to a radio talk show host?"

"Oh, I never have. My parents always said that phrase, and all of the kids picked it up. But really, what will be the rest of your story?"

"I don't have a clue. Fox, can you put suntan lotion on my back, please? I -- Buddy, NO!" Both parents jumped up, but not before there little tyke fell face first into the water.

Instead of crying, he came up laughing. "More," he said. "More."

Fox had already reached him, and planted him back on his feet, but Buddy, or Sal as he was being called more often these days, wanted more lake fun so he sat right down in the waves lapping at the shore.

Ivy marveled at the lack of fear in Buddy. "I think we'd better get him into a toddler swim class for safety. Then at least he can learn to hold his breath, roll onto his back, and float. I'd hate to think of what might happen if he ever wandered away from us. Promise me, you'll always be vigilant around him, Fox."

"I wouldn't do anything less than you would. More even, if that's possible. I love this little guy." He picked up his son and planted a kiss on his chubby cheek.

"Well, I guess we should head back to the house. It's past time for his nap. Maybe with the fresh air and water activity, he'll doze off quickly."

"Oh, does that mean we can have some time to ourselves?" Fox raised an eyebrow in that seductive way he had.

"I think it can be arranged," she giggled. How could she ever deny him anything, Ivy wondered? He was everything to her. She would give him whatever he wanted, whenever he wanted it. She would never take her precious family for granted.

$$\approx$$

"Fox, really, we can't stay in bed all afternoon. I usually take the time when Buddy is sleeping to get things done."

"Like what?" He moved in closer and nuzzled her neck.

"Like the dishes."

"I'll do them. Check."

"Well, like, the laundry."

"I already threw the load into the machine that you had in the basket. It just needs to move to the dryer. Two seconds."

"Well, how about folding Buddy's clothes from the last load?"

"That can be your job. I'm no good at folding. What, five minutes?"

"Well, there's – there's." Ivy began breathing heavier as Fox trailed his fingers over her breasts. All excuses she had come up with were gone from her mind, as Fox began to work his magic on her body. Soon, only soft moans and rustling sheets could be heard from Buddy's parents' room. And then the whole house slept for another hour.

"Where're you going?" he asked with slurred speech.

"To the bathroom."

"K." His face was buried in the pillow. She took a moment to look at her husband's body stretched out on top of the covers. He was a fine specimen of the male form – trim and firm in all the right places. Ivy exhaled deeply, and smiled to herself. She was completely sated and feeling on top of the world. They'd been married almost a year, but they still couldn't keep their hands off of each other. She hoped that would never change, but if it did, there was always the ruby necklace. It was hidden in the secret spot in the bedroom floor for now, and used only on special occasions, because at this point there was no need for an incentive for their lovemaking. Ivy often wondered if it was sending out waves of its aphrodisiac powers through the floorboards, because her need for him was so great. She couldn't imagine having these feelings for anyone other than Fox. How did women go from one man to the next? How did women cheat on their mates? How were men able to have feelings for another and lie over and over again about it to their wives? The only explanation could be that they had never found the right partner in life in the first place.

After washing up and combing her hair, Ivy was fully dressed and ready to continue with the day. She'd let Fox sleep until he was ready to get up. He worked hard, physically, on his time away from his work as a home inspector. There was always something to do around the house. Lately, he had been building a gazebo for the top of the rise before the water's edge. Business was going well for him, and the income was very nice. He had stressed to Ivy that she was not required to work outside of the home, and that writing was all she had to do now, and only if she wanted to continue with it. And she definitely did. She was fulfilling her life's dream, and she was able to stay at home and raise her son at the same time. What could be better?

But without a new storyline, she was at a loss. There were no words needing to be typed, and there was no research needing to be done. She felt adrift and disconnected from her imaginary worlds. She reached for her latest book, Maisy and Max, and ran her fingers over the beautiful cover. Would she ever be able to do this again? So far she only had two books published, but if a new storyline never came to her, that might be it. More than one author had become famous after only one or two books, and then no one had ever heard from them again. They had lost their muse, they liked to say. Was that where she was now? Without a muse?

Her last two books were based on facts. First her great-grandmother, Ruby, had inspired her with her story of prohibition, and Ivy had written 'Ruby and Sal.' And then a strange woman named Gina had approached her in the Frauenthal Theater in Muskegon, and the next thing Ivy knew she had found a fourth cousin, had completed a family tree she had previously known nothing about, and was writing 'Maisy and Max.' Both books were completely out of her hands. They seemed to take on a life of their own.

But now those stories were finished – put to bed, as they say in the publishing industry.

Ivy ran her fingers over the keyboard of her laptop. Nothing! No words, no thoughts, no ideas whatsoever. She slapped the lid shut, disgusted with herself. Oh well, she thought, maybe another day. Her son was moving around in his crib, and her husband had just coughed, a sign he was rising, also. Both were sounds and reminders that there was more to life than just writing a silly story.

Chapter Two

"Ivy, slow down. You're going to wear yourself out before anyone gets here."

"But I want everything to be just perfect, don't you? It's our first family gathering at the cottage."

"Yes, and one of many Fourth of July celebrations here on the lake. So relax. You know all of my family, now. They're not judgmental in any way. They'll come ready to pitch in and help with whatever needs to be done."

Ivy sighed, then bit her lip. "I just wanted all of the decorations to be done, and the tables set up. We can carry out the food when they arrive."

Fox had to chuckle. She was so nervous. Family was everything to her, but what she had not figured out yet was that his family absolutely adored her. She could literally do nothing wrong. "Look, all we need to do is finish putting up the Edison lights. I'll continue to string them from tree to tree. You go inside and clean up the kitchen. And I know you'll need a little time to yourself to get dressed, right? I'll watch Buddy. Plop him in the play yard. Now, go!" He made a shooing motion with his hands.

"Okay, okay. I'm going. But don't forget the TiKi torches. Oh, and stack some wood by the firepit so we can make s'mores around a campfire later."

"Yes, dear," he said mockingly.

Fox was learning how fussy Ivy could be about certain things. Attention to detail was something she had always done well in her job at the department store, but here in the wooded setting at the lake, casual was the word of the day. He knew as soon as his mom and sisters arrived, they would dig right in and take over any chores that were left undone. In fact, they looked forward to it. It was all part of the holiday ritual.

No sooner had Ivy come back outside, freshly showered and dressed in her holiday red, white, and blue outfit, than the cars and vans began to roll into the driveway. Doors opened and kids tumbled out, heading straight to the lake. Mothers yelled, "Don't go in the water. It's too early."

"Hey," called out Fox, "did you come in a caravan? Everyone arrived at the same time."

"As a matter of fact, we did," said his brother-in-law, Jarrod. "It was easier for those who had not been here before." Jarrod leaned in to whisper to Fox, "Your dad drives like a maniac. It was hard to keep up."

"Yeah, he always did have a lead foot." He slapped Jarrod on the back and made a face of horror. "Mom, let me help you with that. But first a hug."

"Oh, Fox, I'm so excited for today. What a special treat to have a family Fourth of July party at a lake."

"And this is the first of many. We want to make it an annual event."

"Well, wait and see if you can stand us all first," responded another brother-in-law, Aaron. "This is the Marzetti clan, you know. They can get a little rowdy. Now, where's that beautiful bride of yours?"

"Take it easy, Aaron. Don't scare her off. We love her too much." Kim, sister number two, piped in and then waved to sister number one. "Sandy, over here. I need your help with this picnic basket. Here, you big lug, take this casserole in. Be careful, it's hot." She shoved it at Aaron. He grinned, kissed her on the cheek, and headed to the house.

Ivy was like a bride in a reception line, receiving kisses and hugs as each family member passed her by. She was overwhelmed with all of the activity and thrilled at the same time. This family was all she had ever dreamed of. They were all so loving and kind. Oh, they had their spats, all right, she had already seen evidence of it on occasion, but they always had each other's backs. They were a strong, solid family. Ivy was so grateful to be a part of it. Before long she was like a master sergeant barking out orders. 'That table goes over there. No, let's place the chairs around the firepit for later. Would someone please get the life jackets out of the boathouse so we can take the kids on a boat ride later?'

Buddy was passed from grandma to aunt and then to another aunt and another, but with this group, he was strictly Sal, short for Salvatore, and sometimes he was called Sally. They never heard the feminine side of that name at all. But whatever name they used, he was eating up all of the attention.

Hours later, when people had settled into the rhythm of eating and swimming and snacking, Ivy collapsed in a chair by the water's edge. Fox's sister, Kim, sat next to her. She reached over and squeezed Ivy's hand. "Thank you for this. It's a perfect day. And you couldn't ask for better weather."

"You're very welcome. I love having you guys here. I'm so happy to be in a big family. You know I didn't have much family growing up."

"Yes, Fox, told me that your mother died when you were young and you were raised by your dad and a grandmother."

"Well, my Dad was only there part time. My grandmother, Olivia, and my great-grandmother, Ruby, actually did most of the raising."

"Oh, Ivy, I wanted to tell you that I read both 'Ruby and Sal' and 'Maisy and Max' back to back. I couldn't put them down. They really are wonderful."

Ivy blushed, still not used to praise about her books. "Thank you, I'm glad you liked them."

"So what's next?"

"I haven't got a clue," sighed Ivy. She was watching as Anne, sister number three, was dunking Sal in the lake up to his waist over and over. He was laughing so hard, that his contagious belly laughs generated her own giggles. Sal's Aunt Sandy was capturing the toddler's antics by making a video on her camera of the whole thing.

"I just love how you worked the family tree into the storyline. Have you done a lot with genealogy before?"

"Not a lot, really. I've tried but it always seemed so confusing. But once I had a few facts about Ruby that were actually true, I was suddenly like a detective on a murder case. I couldn't quit until I solved it."

Kim laughed. "I think you've got the bug. That's what genealogy does to you. And once bitten, you'll never get over it."

"It sounds like you've done a lot of family tree work."

"I have, actually. I worked the Marzetti clan until I couldn't go any further, and then Aaron and I went to Italy to track the villages where they all lived. It was so much fun, and I felt such a connection, so when we returned I started to work on my mother's side."

"The Fox line?" asked Ivy, knowing her husband was named after his mother's maiden name.

"Well, I started there, but I soon got sidetracked by the Ukrainian line."

"Ukrainian? That's new to me. I had no idea."

"Well, we didn't know much either, until I started to dig. And luckily my grandmother is still alive and was able to give me some details to help me get started."

"Where does this part of the family fit in to the Fox line?"

"Mom, Susie keeps splashing me!" whined a little five-year-old girl.

"Then get out of the water if you don't like it. That's what the lake is for – having fun. Sorry about that, Ivy. Let's see. It's a little complicated, because my grandmother married a Fox, but her maiden name is Karpenko; she said her father was an immigrant from the Ukraine in the early 1900s."

"Oh, that's interesting. Have you gone any further than that?"

"Not really. Just a few generations. It was tough because of various wars there over the years, so most church records were destroyed in bombings, etc. I actually paid a genealogist overseas to work on it for me, but we didn't really have any success"

"Wow, you're really into this, aren't you? I'd love to learn more."

"I'd gladly teach you. I can even give you access to the family tree online so you can see for yourself. Oh-oh, it looks like Sally's crying for his momma."

"Yeah, I'd better take care of that. Thanks so much, Kim. Let's pick up this talk later."

The rest of the day was filled with water balloon fights, corn hole toss, and roasting hot dogs over the open fire. Even with all of the casserole dishes that were passed around, they still found room for s'mores. Then, as soon as the sun dipped low on the horizon, the skies lit up with the lake association's fireworks. Buddy cried as his mother held her hands over his ears, but the rest of the crowd added oohs and aahs in chorus, laughing and clapping at the spectacular display. It wasn't long before Buddy began to enjoy the colorful display himself, fascinated with the sparkles and whistles.

The kids slept in sleeping bags on the floor of the cottage, some adults slept in the vans and campers they had brought, while the grandparents took over the coveted guest room. In the morning the rowdiness started all over again, as bacon and eggs were cooked over the open fire. At the end of the weekend, Ivy and

Fox collapsed on the sofa, their son tucked in bed for the night. They were exhausted from all of the commotion and activity.

"What did you think, Mrs. Marzetti?"

"Of--?"

"Of your first family Fourth of July party?"

"I loved every single minute."

"Would you do it again next year?"

"Absolutely. Maybe even Labor Day this year."

"Well, let me have a few days to think about that. I need to recuperate from this party first," said Fox. He was so pleased with how his wife had handled everything, but when he saw the worry line on her forehead, he knew she was mulling over something else, most likely her next book. A dog with a bone, that's what she was. She would never let go.

Chapter Three

She stared at the monitor, her fingers poised gracefully over the keyboard ready to tap out the first sentence, but her hands wouldn't cooperate. Nothing came to her at all. Not even one word. 'How did I ever manage to write the last two books?' she thought. 'I'm not a writer!'

Fox walked out of the bedroom, fresh from his morning shower. His manly soap and shampoo emitted a pine spice and woods combination that was too much to ignore. She smiled to herself.

"What's going on? And why the sexy smile?" He kissed her lightly on the lips before he walked into the kitchen to fill his mug with coffee.

"I was just thinking that you looked and smelled so good I would have no trouble at all if I were an erotic writer." Ivy loved flirting with her husband, but she inevitably ended up embarrassing herself.

Fox laughed. "I can tell by the red blotch on your neckline and the blush on your cheeks that you would be too shy to ever show anyone what you had written. But if you don't mind, maybe you could write something just for me sometime. I'd love to critique it." He followed up that last remark with a wicked grin.

"Oh, stop. You're distracting me," she giggled. "I'm not getting anywhere so far this morning, and if I don't get a few words down, soon Buddy will need some attention and then it will be all over for the day."

"Well, sorry, I can't help, because I have to run. I'm almost late as it is. I've got an early appointment and then another inspection immediately following that one."

"Both in the area, or are you driving far today?"

"Not far, both are West Michigan near the lakeshore. First North Muskegon and then Fruitport."

"Well, enjoy the day. I'll probably still be here when you get back, with not one word on the page." She blew out a breath directed toward her forehead, an old habit of frustration she had developed one year when she had allowed the beautician to cut bangs, which it turned out later she hated. She had had to wait a whole year for them to get back to the proper length, and the whole time they were always irritatingly in her eyes.

"Well, I'll just step over by the Pack 'n Play and give *Sal* a kiss goodbye, then I'm coming back to you. I want more than a little peck this time."

Her eyes followed her husband. She delighted in the way he treated their son. They absolutely adored each other. She would never forgive herself for withholding Buddy from Fox for the first few months of his life. Luckily, if they never brought it up, the baby would never know. As soon as their love had been proven to be strong, they got married in a quick and private ceremony at the court house, but true to the Fox family traditions, the reception was anything but quiet. Ivy had met every single relative on both sides of his family at a hall they had rented in Bay City where Fox was from. There were so many people that she was positive she would never learn their names. And little Sal, or Buddy as she stilled called him, was passed from person to person, bounced on knees and cuddled and played with all afternoon, to his delight. Ivy had not had to change a diaper or clothing all day. Sometimes she even lost track of him, and didn't care, because she knew these wonderful people were taking good care of him.

Fox came back to her and lifted her from her chair, pulling her in close. "Let's never be one of those couples who plant a quick kiss on their spouse's cheek and run out the door. What do you say?"

"I agree. Of course, it does make it difficult to separate and go on with the day, once you've wound me up." She leaned in as he placed his lips on hers for a good long time, while pressing his body to her curves. Ivy was always amazed at how quickly her desire for him was aroused, but this morning she pushed him away gently. "Now, off to work with you, husband. Bring home the bacon, because apparently I won't be making any money for a while."

"Don't worry, hon. Something will come to you. You're a creative person. Just relax and let it happen. Don't try to force it, because if you do it won't be any good, anyway."

"You're so wise." She slapped him on the butt. "Now, go to work and leave me to my misery."

As soon as he walked out the door, Sal began to fuss. He had dropped a toy over the side and it was out of his reach. Now that he was walking, the play area in which she had restricted him wasn't to his liking, making it much more difficult for Ivy to write. She tried to sit down to write whenever he napped, but she was tired then, too, and the words wouldn't come. Recently she had begun getting up when it was still dark, so she could have some quiet time. It had worked for a few days. She actually wrote a short story, but it was not worthy of publishing. And then it seemed like her child caught on to her alone time and decided he would join her. Perhaps she would have to give up family time when Fox was home; he could take their son out for a while by himself, but she knew she would be wishing to be with them the whole time. Maybe she could go to the library for some quiet. If they were out of sight, it might work. Yes, she decided, that was what she was going to do. When Fox came home, she would be the one to go off by herself. On nice days she could even write in the park. Just thinking of a plan, gave her more incentive. She closed the laptop and tended to her son. She would write later.

≈

Leaving the lake and his family was the most difficult part of the day for Fox. If it were up to him he would stay home all the time. He loved nothing better than puttering around his house and playing with Sal. Fox had always known he wanted a family someday, but he had surprised himself with the love and devotion he felt for the two newest people in his life. He could honestly say he had never been happier.

Forcing himself to think about the job before him, he began to go into home inspector mode. He knew he was going to meet someone at a North Muskegon house, but he had not been given the name of the owner, just the mortgage company and the address. He pulled up to an older home on Muskegon Lake, one of those real beauties that he had often dreamed about owning. Each house had such charm and elegance, and of course the view was spectacular. In the old days when the ships were coming through the channel from Lake Michigan into Muskegon Lake, loaded with iron ore for the foundries or delivering logs for the paper mill, these homes provided a spectacular sight for ship watching. It was just recently that the last ship went through the channel as the paper mill had closed and the foundries were no longer functioning. Things had changed a lot in Muskegon; it now leaned towards the tourist industry, with new shops and hotels popping up every day on the south side of the lake.

Some of these lake homes, previously built by lumber barons and factory magnates, could qualify as mansions, and it was one of these grand old structures that Fox would be using his skills on today. It would most likely take much longer than he had originally thought, so after parking the car but before entering the house, he placed a call to cancel his next appointment and then he called Ivy to tell her would be home late. She was disappointed, of course, but she understood what his job entailed. He never dreamed, when he first hung out his shingle and went into business for himself, that he would be so successful in such a short amount of time. His reputation had preceded him as he had formerly worked for a firm that had secured a lot of inspections and appraisals in this area.

Since there was not another car in the driveway, he surmised that no one else was present, so he began his inspection by walking around the home, taking measurements, checking out the foundation, and taking a visual of the roof from below. He would need to go up on a ladder to closer inspect the age and condition of the shingles. He was hard at work in just a few minutes, when he heard a car pull up and then the motor turn off. He walked around the front to greet his client and introduce himself. The view he was awarded with was quite a surprise. A female wearing a short skirt, was exposing her behind as she reached for something in the back seat. She displayed a nicely rounded bottom covered in the smallest of lacy panties, well-toned thighs, and long legs free of nylons. One foot was gracefully balanced in the air and attached to a pair of very high heels. He took a moment to enjoy the view, lost in his fantasy, until he thought of Ivy. He shook his head to get back on track, thinking to himself as an explanation for his temporary lack of judgement, 'I might be married, but I'm not dead.' It was the standard line all men used when covering for their wandering eyes.

Fox cleared his throat and called out a greeting, "Hello. I'm your home inspector."

She jumped, cracked her head on the top of the door opening, and then swore, as she dropped her iPad on the floor of the car. "Oops, sorry. That slipped out, just like this elusive tablet." When she raised her head, her dark hair spilling over her face, Fox detected something familiar, and an alarm went off. He tensed, hoping it was not true.

She stood upright, and began to extend her hand, but then stopped in her tracks. "Well, well. I guess no introductions are needed, are they?"

"Piper! Piper Evans? Wow, it's been a long time," he stuttered. She moved slowly forward and wrapped her arms around him. She smelled the same, she felt the same, and amazingly, she hadn't aged a day since he had last seen her almost twenty years ago. Still beautiful, still sensual, and so put together. She had it all and she knew how to use it. She kissed his cheek, but it was more of a caress than a peck, as her hand gently touched his face. He could tell that she was inhaling his aftershave; she lingered a bit too long. Fox was normally calm and collected, but for some reason now that he was a married man, this chance encounter threw him.

"Why, Fox, are you blushing? I don't believe I ever thought that was possible."

"No, I was just caught off guard, that's all. I'm in my professional mode, and you set me back to another time, I guess. How are you, Pipe?"

"I'm fabulous, and I can see you are doing well. You still have that gorgeous curl that just won't stay put. How many women have wanted to put it back in place, I wonder?"

He cleared his throat. "I'd rather not say exactly, but you were always different," he laughed. "If it wasn't on my forehead, you would pull it down."

"Because it made you look so sexy," she purred. "And it still does."

Fox cleared his throat. "Well, yes. Now about the house."

"What? No small talk? Maybe later, hm?" She smiled coyly; she had always been a great flirt. She linked her arm in his and led him to the front door. She swayed her hips just enough so they gently bumped into his. The contact was electric. "Let's go inside, shall we?"

Chapter Four

The drive home was troublesome for Fox, as he thought over the events of the day. He had managed to keep Piper at a respectable distance, even though he could tell she wanted more. There was no guessing about it; she had made it perfectly clear that she was available if he so chose. He had told her he was married, and she had raised an eyebrow in surprise, then simply said, "Really." When he tried to tell her about Ivy, she had ignored him and hinted at something she said she had to tell him instead, but he had changed the subject a few times to avoid intimate conversation. They were in the house alone for more than two hours, and even though things had been over between them long ago, the attraction was still strong. He kept himself at a safe distance at all times. Even so, when he caught her staring at him, and when he watched her catlike movements, always so slow and deliberate, he was unnerved. He was a married man now and deeply in love with his wife, so he couldn't understand why he still had these feelings. He felt like a bumbling college kid all over again. Maybe he was unhinged because of the way things had ended between them. It had been a painful time for Fox, and one he would rather not remember.

There was a time when he had been over-the-moon in love with Piper. She came from a wealthy Grosse Point family, and she had been given everything she had ever wanted. When the other girls in school were struggling to keep up with their grades and work at the same time, always exhausted and looking the worst for wear at times, Piper had all the clothes and makeup she wanted. She would often leave campus for a mani/pedi, or to get her hair cut in the latest fashion. There was no need for her to work, so there was plenty of time to fuss with her appearance, and she was brilliant besides, therefore the classes all came easily to her. She was in fact, perfect in every way in Fox's eyes.

He had watched her for a while from afar, afraid to ever think she could be interested in someone like him. But he forgot one thing. He was a jock, not the captain of the football team but still an excellent player and someone the scouts were watching, and he was good-looking to boot. He had never had any trouble getting a girl before, but for some reason Piper Evens had always seemed unattainable – until she laid eyes on him at a frat party, and once Piper made up her mind that she wanted something, she got it.

Fox usually didn't care for aggressive girls, but it was Piper, the girl every man on campus wanted. Once she beckoned, he followed like a lost puppy dog. He was no longer the one in control. The guys, of course, thought it was great, and cheered him on for his great catch. They didn't seem to notice that he was the one who had been caught – caught in a web of lies and deceit, as it would turn out later. So with all of the turmoil that had surrounded their relationship, Fox could not understand his feelings today. His heart had raced at the sight of her, his breath had quickened, his lips had suddenly gone dry, and when she had caressed his face and kissed his cheek, he felt a manly stirring he was ashamed of.

Before getting out of the car to greet Ivy and his son, Fox sat for a few minutes to compose himself. Why he was so nervous, was difficult to understand, because of course, Ivy would never know what had happened today. And actually nothing had happened, since he had managed to keep Piper at arm's length. But she requested another meeting after the work he had suggested that was needed to be done was completed – to be sure it was done properly, she had said. She was going to buy the house outright with cash, so she would not be going through a bank. The inspections were purely for her own peace of mind. She had even hinted that perhaps more than two meetings might be needed. Fox would make sure that Ivy did not know about these appointments; there was no way she would ever know, anyway. He never discussed his clients and their purchases with her. The only reason he would go back was because he needed the money, and Piper had very influential friends who could help his business. That's what he told himself. Taking a deep breath, he grabbed his briefcase, and went into the house to his warm and loving wife. Maybe tonight they could cuddle by the fire, and he would reassure himself that his love for her was strong.

≈

"Fox, you're just in time for dinner. Perfect timing, as a matter of fact." Ivy smiled warmly at her husband and then went into his arms for their customary kiss hello. Usually it was more of a peck, but today Fox wrapped his arms around her as he held her tightly then followed with a very sensual kiss. His hands roamed over her backside and then up and around to her front. "Fox, what is going on?" giggled Ivy, gently pushing his hands away. "Sal is right there."

"What, don't you want our son to know how much his father loves his mother?" he said in a sexy growl, as he pulled her back in and nibbled her neck.

"Well, yes, but not quite this way. Besides, he's waiting for his hug and kiss, too. Would you deny a boy who worships you?"

"Never!" he laughed, then he turned to his son and lifted him high in the air. Sal giggled as he called out "Dada, higher! Higher!"

'Yes,' thought Fox. 'This is what life is all about. This is what I want.' Then he turned to his beautiful wife and said, "What's for dinner?"

≈

Later in the evening, when their darling bundle of joy had worn them out and was now sleeping soundly in his bed for the night, the couple chatted about their day. Fox downplayed his inspection, just saying he needed to return for another visit.

"It could be something good for business. This particular client has a lot of influence with the rich and famous," he said, making air quotes. "Someday soon I might be able to add another piece of jewelry to compliment your ruby and diamond necklace."

"Oh, Fox, I hope you know I don't need anything like that. I have everything I've ever dreamed of right here in this house – my great-grandmother's cottage. I think she always knew that things would work out for me here, and that's why she told me her story. It set me on the path to being an author, and at the same time brought me happiness."

Fox kissed her on the forehead and stroked her arm. "How is the book writing coming along?"

Ivy sighed, settling into the circle of his arm. "Nothing yet. I can't think of a single thing to write about. I'm thinking about taking a break and trying to get back to my genealogy hobby. I can't seem to find time to do both, and maybe this will give me a bit of a breather, so I won't be so stressed out about a new storyline."

"Whatever you think is best. You know you are not required to write. You should only do it if it pleases you. I want you to be happy."

"But writing makes me happy, that's what's so troubling. I should be able to come up with something. I've never had writer's block before." Ivy pouted, causing a small crease line to appear on her forehead. "I was thinking about contacting your sister, Kim, about your family tree and looking into your ancestry. I think she's done quite a bit already, but I might be able to add a few more names to the branches."

"That's a wonderful idea! And Kimmy would love it; you know she's crazy about you. She said right from the beginning that you were perfect for me. She's always been a big supporter of yours as far as the books go, too."

"So, you wouldn't mind if I start to poke around in your family's background?"

Fox beamed. "Not at all. It sounds like fun. Well, not for me, but I look forward to seeing what else you can find. Names and dates are not my thing, but I know Kim is always talking about one branch or another."

"Good, I'll call her tomorrow. Maybe she can send me what she has so far, or let me access her tree online. I purchased a genealogy account as part of my research for the last two books, so it was a write-off. I still have almost six months left on my subscription. Yes, I'm excited now!"

"Good, well let's take some of that excitement to the bedroom. I've been waiting for you all day."

"I'd like nothing better," Ivy whispered. In their passion, the couple was not even aware that the necklace was vibrating underneath the floorboard next to their bed, but if they had not been so busy, they would have noticed a red glow showing through the cracks.

Chapter Five

"Morning, Kim. Have you got time to talk?"

"Sure, I just sent the kids off to school, so I'm good for a few hours. You might hear water running and dishes clinking, though, while I try to clean up the breakfast mess." To the outside world, Kim's life might look crazy and over-the-top busy, but she loved every minute of it and wouldn't change a thing for 'all the tea in China,' as she loved saying. "When you're a stay-at-home mom, you might look to everyone else in the work force as someone who has lots of free time once the kids go off for the day, but in reality that's when the work is just beginning. Although I do admit to taking breaks now and then with a good book or a cup of my favorite java."

"And why not? You deserve it, right? And besides, if you were working at a job outside the home, you would get a coffee break every two hours."

Kim laughed out loud. "That's exactly the way I think. Although I don't get a break every two hours, I try to get at least one in the day plus lunch. If I didn't take that time, I'd be brain dead as well as physically useless when they come home from school."

Ivy smiled at the thought that someday that life would be hers. As soon as Sal was ready to go to school, she would be the one running around to soccer games and band practice. Maybe there would be another son or daughter in the family by then, also, causing even more chaos, but bringing with him or her more laughter and love. "I won't keep you long, but I wanted to ask you about something you had mentioned on The Fourth of July."

"What's that? That my little brother has a perfect life with a gorgeous woman and a sweet child he loves deeply, *and* at the same time he lives on a lake? Oh, that's right, I never said that out loud. I might have sounded jealous." Kim snorted at her own joke.

"Actually, no, that wasn't it. But thank you very much for painting a picture of my paradise. And you know you're welcome here anytime at my lake house."

"Thanks, Ivy. Fox has extended the invitation many times, and we'll take him up on it soon, but what can I help you with this morning?"

"I was thinking about something you said at the picnic about your family tree. You have completed the whole Marzetti side back as far as you can go, right?"

"Yes, I do. I've been working on it for years. You're welcome to a copy, if you want to keep it for little Sal someday. The Italian side is quite interesting."

Ivy grinned on her end of the phone. "That would be wonderful! Can you send it to me through email?"

Always eager to talk genealogy, Kim was more than willing to share her research. "Of course. I can get that out to you later today. Are you getting ready to dig into our mysterious family?"

"Honestly, that's exactly what I want to do. I need a hobby other than writing. I'm having a little bit of a dry spell, and I need some sort of distraction for a bit to relax me. But what do you mean about mysterious?"

"Well, as I said, our grandmother is of Ukrainian descent. We just don't know enough about that. I sure wished you lived closer. I have a start on that line, but I never have time to work on it anymore. It's the one branch I'm stuck on. I can send what I have, although I only go back a few generations, just what Grandma has told us, and she doesn't know much. The biggest thing is there is a box of letters and some pictures that are in her possession that have been passed on from her mother, but the letters are all in Ukrainian or Polish or Russian or something. With the Cyrillic script, I can't read a word of it. It's been puzzling me for years. My grandmother can understand some of the spoken language, but she doesn't read it, so we're stuck."

"I'd love to take a shot at it. That might be just the kind of puzzle I've been looking for," said Ivy eagerly.

Kim thought a moment. "Do you have Ancestry.com access?"

"Yes, I have a subscription."

"Wonderful. I'll give you access to my family tree, and then you can view everything I have without going through email."

"That would be perfect, Kim. Thanks so much!"

"Not a problem. It could be fun, working together on this. You've got my family tree juices flowing again. I'm going to dig up any other odds and ends I have and see what else I can come up with for you, and – oops, I'm getting another call. It's the school. I'd better get it."

"Okay. Thanks so much. Loved talking to you."

The line was instantly disconnected without Kim saying goodbye. Kids came first with her, no matter who was left hanging on the other end of the line.

≈

Ivy went about her day taking care of Buddy, as she still liked to call him, paying bills online and doing some laundry. She took joy in the simple tasks, and thanked God for giving her this wonderful life with Fox. She had the family she had always longed for, she was a published author, and she had a man she loved beyond all reason. Life was perfect.

Every few hours Ivy would go to the computer to see if Kim had forwarded her the link to the ancestry site. Once the thoughts of a new genealogy line had started, she had begun to get excited to see if there was anything she could offer. Sometimes brick walls were just that, and no one could break through them.

And true to her word, later that day, Kim sent her family tree link to Ivy's email. Sal was down for a nap, and so it gave Ivy some free time to explore the family line. First she scrolled through the Marzetti clan, but it was very detailed, going back many generations through the United States and then through Italy. Not much she could add there. Then Ivy began to look through Fox's mother's line. It began with Kim, of course, because she was the one who had done it, but since she was Fox's sister the line was the same from that point on. Patricia Fox was born in 1955 in Petoskey, and married Antonio Enrico Marzetti in Bay City. Ivy knew her father-in-law as Hank, but she could see that *his* father was also an Antonio. They probably didn't want two Tony's in the family; therefore, he was called Hank. Hank would have been a nickname for Henry which was American for Enrico. Patricia's father's name was Samuel Fox, born in 1932, and her mother's name was Kataryna Karpenko, born 1933.

"Ah," said Ivy out loud. "There's the Ukrainian line." Biting her lip in concentration she continued on, but the line ended after only one more generation.

Kataryna's parents were Anton Karpenko and Yulia, who were Fox's great-grandparents. She decided to wait until Fox came home and ask if he had ever known these people, and if so if he had any memory of them. She spent the rest of the afternoon researching anything and everything about Ukraine and its people, and discovered a very interesting culture she had never known anything about.

Ivy could hear Buddy stirring in the other room. She saved her link to a file so she could return to it another day. She couldn't wait until she could get back to Kim's line and try to continue with her own research; she hadn't been this excited since she had begun working on Maisy and Max.

Chapter Six

The sun was a dazzling ball of fire framed by a periwinkle blue sky, but despite the cheery weather, Fox felt as gloomy as the color grey. He emerged from the car, with shoulders slumped, and began walking slowly toward the house. He prayed Ivy would not be able to read his mind. He had spent the day at the North Muskegon mansion again, and even though Piper said she would not be there, she had shown up, just the same, with some lame excuse. She had explained that she had wanted to measure for drapes and area rugs, and it was the only time she could make it during the week. Fox was positive she had arranged to be at the house at the exact time he was, and he was also sure that she had an ulterior motive. She had hinted once again at needing a private talk, but even though they were completely alone in the house, she never got around to stating what she wanted to talk to him about. He wasn't certain of what she was up to, but he knew one thing – she was definitely making a play for him again. He chatted constantly about Ivy, bringing up his wife's name whenever possible and bragging about her books and the success she had had, but nothing deterred Piper. She was not the least bit fazed with the fact that he was married. She made certain to brush up against him, often getting so close that her breast stroked his arm. Once she came from behind pointing at something she had a question about, as she leaned far enough forward so that she was whispering in his ear in her soft raspy voice. Fox backed away immediately, but she was beginning to have a very dangerous effect on him, and he was truly concerned. He had never thought of himself as a weak man, but where Piper was concerned, he was like a moth to a flame, and that flame would surely burn up everything good about his life if he let it. She had done it to him before, and she could do it again. On the drive home, he made a vow to give up that account for the sake of his marriage, even if it meant giving up the referrals that were sure to come. Nothing was more important to him than Ivy. Nothing.

Before he turned the knob, he put on a bright smile; he wanted to be sure Ivy did not suspect that he had something heavy on his mind. He would have to tell her about his past and how it had come to invade their life, but not now, because he did not want to see pain in Ivy's eyes. There would be time if he was careful and played it right. He could break the story about his past slowly and beg for forgiveness. But for now, he wanted to enjoy the wonderful family he had. He put on a bright smile, and opened the door to the cottage. "Hi, I'm home."

"Oh Fox, there you are! I'm so glad. I have so much to tell you."

"Come into my arms, first, woman. I missed you."

Ivy melted into his warm embrace. She would never take this man for granted. In her eyes, he deserved to be on a pedestal as a fine example of what every husband should be.

"Dada. Dada."

Fox was attacked at knee level by a mini lookalike. He pick his son up and tickled his belly, then he twirled him around in a circle.

"How was your day, honey?" asked Ivy as she walked back to the kitchen

Fox hesitated and then said, "Pretty average, I'd say. I think I'm done with the house in North Muskegon. So on to the next project "

"Oh, that's good. Do you have another job lined up, already?"

"Not yet, but I will, I'm sure." Fox would not let Ivy feel his concerns. If he didn't handle Piper with kid gloves, she had the power to destroy him. "So, what's your exciting news?"

"I talked to Kim today."

"That's exciting? Your life must be pretty boring for you to get worked up about talking to my big sister," he laughed.

Ivy turned around from the stove, sporting a big grin on her face. "You think you're so funny. Actually, Kim sent me the family tree file and gave me access to her Ancestry site so I can pop in on it whenever I want. She sure has done a lot on the Marzetti clan. There are so many branches on the Italian family tree, I could barely follow it."

"So how does that help you?"

"She gave me permission to dig into your mother's side."

"Really? You mean the Foxes?" Fox was barely listening as most men do. He pretended to be paying attention while his mind was elsewhere -- back at the mansion and the problem with a past he might have to share.

Ivy could tell she was losing his interest, so she simply stated, "Well, it starts with your mother marrying a Fox, but before that she came from Ukrainian descent. I want to explore *that* line."

"Oh yes, my Grandma Kat. You would have met her at the wedding reception, but she had bronchitis and they were afraid it would go into pneumonia, so she had to stay home. Hey, that gives me an idea! Since you've never met her, let's take a day trip to Petoskey. I'm sure she'd get a kick out of meeting Sal, too."

"Oh, I didn't realize that's where she lived. I thought I heard something about a lake called Loon Lake?"

"Almost, she actually lives on *Walloon* Lake near Petoskey. And it gets even better. Her family has had a cottage there for several generations. They were neighbors of the Hemingways back in the day – still are.

Some family members still live there. Maybe you'll get inspired there for your next book."

"Really? You mean *Ernest* Hemingway?" Ivy raised her eyebrows so high Fox had to laugh.

"The one and only. An unforgettable man."

"I knew he spent time in Michigan, but I had no idea he came from Petoskey. I'd be thrilled to be anywhere near the area that he lived. Maybe Ernest's genius will rub off."

"I'll tell you what. We'll take a driving tour and stop at his old haunts. We could even stay overnight if you want to. Gram's always asking one of us kids to visit. She's a bundle of energy. You'll love her, and she can fill you in on as much history as you need."

"Oh, Fox, this is perfect! When can we leave?"

"Let me call her and make sure she doesn't have any plans, then we'll mark it on the calendar. I'll rearrange my work schedule to fit."

Ivy seductively moved to her man, then she wound her arms around his neck. "What did I ever do to deserve you?"

≈

Slowly stretching her arms above her pillow, a secret smile played on Ivy's lips. A very sensual feeling overcame her and traversed the length of her body. She blushed to herself as she was reminded of the night before. She ran her hands down her hips and over her smooth, taut stomach, remembering Fox's touch, then she moved her hand toward her sleeping husband, only to discover an empty cool sheet. He wasn't in bed with her, apparently having risen much earlier. There were no sounds coming from the kitchen, so he could not be making breakfast. The baby's room was also alarmingly quiet. Ivy sat up with a start, wondering what time it was. She focused her blurry eyes on the clock next to the bed. 10:00!! She had not slept this late in years. Ivy jumped out of bed, needing to check on her son immediately. A quick check of his room, revealed nothing but an empty crib. Dirty dishes in the sink showed that her men had already eaten breakfast. Placing her hand on the glass carafe, Ivy felt the coffee pot. It had turned itself off automatically, but the pot was still lukewarm. She poured herself a cup since it was the temperature she liked anyway, then walked to the patio door to look outside. Sure enough, Fox was standing on the dock with their little boy in his arms, pointing at the ducks and early morning fishing boats gently bobbing on the water.

The lake looked like a reflecting glass, with only a small wake moving behind a single rowboat. Little tufts of mist rose up on the opposite shore near the clumps of cattails. Ivy thought she had never seen anything so beautiful as the picture displayed before her of her two favorite men with the gorgeous lake as a background. She sighed as she leaned against the door jam, coffee cup in hand.

Fox seemed to sense her watching them, because he slowly turned toward her. At the same moment Sal began waving his chubby arms, calling, "Mama. Mama." As he walked toward the house, she heard Fox call out, "Sleepyhead! You're awake."

Once Fox reached the porch and Ivy, he wrapped her in a big bear hug, snuggling their toddler in between them. Ivy inhaled his outdoorsy maleness and marveled at the contrast of the sweet scent of her male child. Life was good, so good, she thought.

"Sorry, I don't know what happened," apologized Ivy. "I never sleep this late."

"Maybe a little too much activity, last night? Hmm?" said Fox with a raised eyebrow and a chuckle. "I'll bet you're starving."

"Ravenous, as a matter of fact."

"I wonder why. Well, I have just the solution. I made pancakes and bacon, and I have some keeping warm in the microwave."

"Really? How do you do that?"

"Come in, sit down, and I'll explain." He led her to the kitchen table and pulled out a chair for her. Then he plopped their son in the highchair. "You see, the microwave is a much smaller space than the room."

Ivy laughed, as he waved his arms making gestures as though he were a science professor in a classroom. "And when you place something that is already hot in this small box and close the door, the heat is contained within, and cannot escape to the larger outside area; therefore it remains warmer for a longer period of time. Voila! Madame, I give you Pancakes au Marzetti."

Now Ivy was laughing so hard her eyes were tearing. "Pancakes *au* Marzetti? Aren't you mixing your French with your Italian?"

"Oui, oui, madame. But for you, anything eese poss-ee-ble."

"Well, thank you, honey, what a treat. I'm so rested, and now breakfast is served. I feel very special."

"And you should, I only wish I could do this all day, but duty does call. I have an inspection nearby and then I should be done, sooooo, I thought if you can have Sal ready when I return, we can take the rest of the weekend off and head to Walloon lake to see Grandma Kat."

"Oh, Fox, that sounds wonderful. Does she know we're coming, though? I wouldn't want to pop in on her unexpectedly."

"Yup. I called her first thing this morning. I knew she was an early riser. And she's more than thrilled at our visit. I'll bet she's already planning a menu. She said we can stay overnight if we want. She has a spare room with a double bed and a crib. She always keeps it at the ready with fresh sheets, just in case."

"Oh, that's sounds wonderful. What can we take along to help out? I can bake some cookies while you're gone, or make my pineapple upside-down cake."

"No, please don't bother. Grandma loves to feed people. You might be stepping on her toes. Just be yourself, and she'll love you." He kissed her on the nose.

"I'm so excited, Fox! I'm going to pack Sal's bag, and I'll do ours, too. I'll have everything ready, so when you come home we can leave. And I'll print out some of the information that Kim sent me so I can discuss family history with her. Maybe I'll learn something new."

"Okay, the little bugger is all yours. I have to leave now. I'm just going to be in Montague, so I shouldn't be too long." He kissed Ivy again, and then bent to kiss his son on the top of the head. "See you later, alligator! High five." He was rewarded with little chubby fingers raising as high as Sal could reach to slap his daddy's hand.

≈

The drive to Montague only took a matter of minutes, and since he was very familiar with the area, Fox knew exactly where to go to find the house. When he pulled up to the address of the ranch-style home, a car was waiting for him in the driveway. He was surprised because he was under the impression that the owner would not be there, and that the key was in the lockbox hanging on the door. At the same time that he emerged from his car, a middle-aged woman in a business suit got out of hers. She had a friendly smile, and as she approached him she extended her hand in introduction.

"Hi, I'm Sue Anders."

"Hello. Fox Marzetti. I thought I would be alone today. Is there a problem?"

"Not really," she laughed, "if you don't want to get in the house, that is." She dangled the keys on her hand. "The last time I was here, I accidentally forgot to replace the key in the box. I was about to return it when you pulled up. So happy to meet you, though." She let her eyes roam over him from top to bottom, making Fox a little uncomfortable. "Piper didn't tell me you were so good looking."

"Piper? What does she have to do with this?"

"She was the one who told me to call you if I needed an inspector for one of my clients' homes. She was very clear that it was hands off, though. Apparently, she wants you all to herself," she sighed. "Too bad, I would have liked to ask you for a drink later this evening, you know, to talk real estate, etc.," she said, smiling flirtatiously.

Fox stiffened. He had not been around anyone other than Piper since he got married who had so overtly come on to him. What was going on? "Well, I'm sorry, Miss Anders –

"Sue, please."

"Miss Anders," Fox said firmly, "I'm married. I don't know what Piper has been saying about me, but we are not a couple. Now, can we keep this professional? I'd like to get on with my work. My *son* is waiting for me to take him on a little trip."

Sue pulled back the keys into her hand, and walked in front of Fox to the front door. She swayed her hips in an exaggerated fashion, but it only put Fox off all the more. She put the key in the lock, then opened the door for him, but she held her ground so he had to walk closely past her in order to get in. "So, where are you taking your son, if I might ask?"

Eager to change the subject, Fox answered, "We're going to Walloon Lake to visit his great-grandmother."

"Oh, it's so pretty there. I just love the Petoskey area." Sue had placed emphasis on the word love and followed it up with a slow lick of her upper lip.

Fox cleared his throat, "Well, I'm good now. Thank you, but I prefer to work alone. I'll return the key to the box when I'm through."

"Sure, sure, I understand. No problem." She sighed. "I'll be on my way, then."

"Oh, one more thing, Miss Anders. Did you ask Piper for a referral?"

"No, she approached me. She said she wanted to help a special friend who was starting a new business. And I'm so glad she did. It was *very* nice meeting you. Here's my card, and if you change your mind about that drink, I can be quite *flexible* -- in my schedule, if you know what I mean. Just give me a call, anytime. I look forward to seeing your -- report." She exhaled loudly, smiled wickedly, and then walked back out to her car.

As soon as he was alone, Fox laughed out loud. "I guess, you've still got it, old boy."

Checking off his list, one item at a time, he made notes about the good and the bad. He was finished in about an hour. He could type up his notes on the laptop from his grandmother's house, and send them through email along with his bill. He had no intention of ever meeting Sue Anders again. But Piper Evans was another story. He did not want her meddling in his business. He could survive just fine without her help. The less he saw of her the better, so perhaps a quick text to tell her to butt out would do the trick. There was no need for social graces with her as far as he was concerned. He had decided that he would rather flounder in his new inspection and appraisal business than depend on her and her friends.

As soon as he was finished, he returned the key to its proper place in the lockbox, made sure the door was secure, and left to be with his family. Grandma Kat was waiting.

Chapter Seven

"Let me see that darling boy." The woman's hands reached out to take Ivy's son out of her arms, but Ivy didn't mind at all. She loved knowing there was family who would love and cherish him the same way she did.

"Grandma, be careful. That's my son you're smothering," laughed Fox.

"Oh, never you mind. A boy can never have too many kisses. Too many people think cuddling is just for girls, but if a boy is going to grow up to be a loving husband, he has to be given affection himself as a child." And Sal *was* loving every minute of it. He instinctively knew that this was a person he could trust. "Now, take your boy back, so I can greet your wife properly." Then she wrapped her arms around Ivy and kissed her on the cheek. "It's wonderful to finally meet the love of Fox's life. So sorry I missed the wedding."

"And I am more than thrilled to meet you. I've heard a lot about you."

"Well, I hope it's all good, but I don't see how it could be," she chuckled. "Now, proper introductions, Fox. Where are your manners?"

Fox grinned from ear to ear. He'd heard this drill from her all of his life. "You've hardly given me a chance, Grandma. Grandma, this is Ivy Morton Marzetti, my wife and the mother of my child. Ivy, this is Kataryna -- known to all as Kat -- Karpenko Fox, my maternal grandmother and the other special lady in my life."

Ivy extended her hand and said formerly, "It's very nice to meet you, Mrs. Fox."

"Oh, for Pete's sake, call me Grandma, or Gram, like everyone else in the family does. Now come, dear, let me get you some coffee or tea. How about some cookies to go with it?"

"Snickerdoodles?" asked Fox with raised eyebrows.

"What else would I make for you, boy?"

Fox clapped his hands in excitement as if he were ten years old. "Let's get to it. I've been eager for my son to try your cookies, which are, by the way, the best I have *ever* had."

She was short and round, but she moved with the speed of lightning, bustling in her kitchen as if she could do it with her eyes closed. Her hair had obviously been combed earlier in the day but gray wisps had escaped, most likely while she worked in her steamy kitchen. Ivy could see the Ukrainian heritage in her features, the rounded face and sharp lines to her nose, the clear blue eyes, which were so different from the Italian Marzettis. Ivy knew she was going to love this woman as if she were her own grandmother. Tears came to her eyes in remembrance of Olivia, her grandmother, and Ruby, her great-grandmother, both gone now. How she missed them.

"So, what did you do in Petoskey before you came here?" asked Grandma Kat.

Fox cleared his throat. "How did you know we were in Petoskey first?"

"Doesn't everyone go there to trace Ernest Hemingway's steps?"

"And we did," laughed Ivy. "It was so much fun. We saw the library building he used to write in, and we even went into the bar and grill where he used to hang out. I sat on his favorite bar stool! The Historic Gaslight District is so quaint. And then we drove through Bay View. Those Victorian homes are absolutely gorgeous. I'd like to spend more time there someday. I think that community would be so inspiring."

"Well, I'm glad you enjoyed yourselves, but you know there were a lot of sides to Hemingway. You can admire his writings, but not his lifestyle. He was quite complicated, in some ways, but when he was here at Walloon Lake for the summers at the home his parents called Windemere, he was just a kid like any other who liked to fish, ride his bike, and cause trouble. He spent 22 years of his life here."

"I've heard that his family cottage was around here somewhere."

"Cream or sugar in your coffee, Ivy?"

"Black, please."

"Wonderful. And a cookie for you, baby," she cooed.

Once all cups were filled, she continued the conversation as if it had never been interrupted. "Yes, his family's cottage is actually just two doors down. My mother knew him well. She was just a year younger than he was. She looked forward to the family coming every summer. She said he was so handsome, even then, and that she had a big crush on him; I always thought they had a thing going on when they were teens. Then when he was eighteen he was off having adventures in World War I. He would write to her on occasion because she had expressed a desire to be a writer herself. I always wondered what happened to those letters. They would be worth a lot of money now."

"Wow, they sure would be. I've always been fascinated by Hemingway's life," said Ivy. "But I have to admit that his writing isn't my style. In the early days it seemed choppy with disconnected sentences, and later when he wrote about war and death, it seemed depressing. But then I guess his writing reflected his own mood, as he became a depressed man once he started to drink heavily."

"Yes, it's sad how he ended his life," said Fox. "Nothing should ever be that horrible that you can't find a way to work through it. Depression, alcohol, and drugs, seemed to have been a family curse. Several members took their own lives."

"That's horrible, isn't it?" Kat was silent a moment, her face reflecting her memories, and then she clapped her hands. "Okay," she said, "let's forget about Hemingway for a while. I want to get to know you better, Ivy. I've heard you're a writer, too."

Ivy was surprised at the change of emotions, but she would later learn that's who Kat Karpenko was. She could spin her thoughts on a dime and change her moods to go with them. Ivy spread a blanket on the floor for little Sal to play on. She put several of his toys next to him, and he was more than happy to sit there for a while, as long as he had a cookie in his mouth.

"Actually," she said with humility, "I like to call myself a writer, and I have been successful with two books so far, but unless I follow up with another and then another again, I can easily fade away into the myriad of writers out there today. And my publisher will drop me in a New York minute. It's so difficult to keep the momentum going. And to make matters worse, I have writer's block," Ivy moaned, her face reflecting the state of her problem.

"What? No new ideas? Look around you, girl. Get inspired the way Hemingway did with the beauty of this place."

"That's what I was hoping to do. Maybe a walk later around the lake will help. Will the owners of Windemere care if I stand on their dock? Maybe I can absorb some of his muse. Or maybe I'll write a book about fishing!"

Grandma Kat laughed. "That won't be a problem. It's still owned by family members. I'll call over and let them know who you are, so they won't be alarmed when they see a stranger out there. They really don't like sightseers hanging around. Some can get a little too aggressive, if you know what I mean."

"I can certainly understand that. It must be hard to maintain their privacy."

Sal stood up and began to toddle away. When Fox went to grab him, he made a face and turned his nose away. "Whoa, little man. That's some smell. What did you eat for breakfast? I think a diaper change is in order. You two go ahead and chat. I've got this."

"Thanks, hon," Ivy blew Fox a kiss and sighed, thinking there was nothing sexier than a man who could take care of his own child.

After a few moments, Fox stuck his head back in the room. "Ivy, did you bring the extra diapers? I thought they were on the counter when we left the house."

"Didn't I put them in the diaper bag?"

"No, there's only one diaper in there. Just enough to solve the current crisis."

"Oh, shoot. Sorry, I thought you had them, I guess. What are we going to do?"

"No problem. As soon as I've cleaned him up, I'll put him down for a nap and run into town. You ladies keep on chatting. It's all under control."

Kat patted Ivy's hand. "You're really lucky to have snagged that one. He's one in a million."

"I realize that, and I'm so thankful for him every day. We almost didn't make it, you know, but that was mostly my fault." Ivy lowered her eyes in embarrassment.

"Well, it takes a good woman to admit that, also. I'm happy for you two. So, what is it that you want to ask about the family? Kim called and gave me a heads up."

"Okay, all set," said Fox. "Sally is down in the crib in the spare room. He seemed pretty drowsy. It won't be long before he's out. Be back in a few." He kissed his lovely wife first and then his grandmother's soft cheek.

"Be careful," the women said in unison, and then they also laughed at the same time, too.

"Now, let's get back to our chat before the little guy needs us. What can I tell you about my family? Oh shoot, there's the phone." Kat turned her back as she spoke into her cell. "Hello? No dear, I can't see you today. Well, yes, you know I told you that my grandson and his wife were coming." She paused to listen to the voice on the other end. "Okay, we'll talk later, I promise. Bye, Duane. Yes, me too."

When Kat turned back to Ivy she had a rosy blush on her cheeks. "Sorry, about that."

"Did we interrupt something with our visit?" asked Ivy.

"No, don't you worry about a thing. It's just Duane. He wanted to take me to lunch, but we can do it another time."

"Hmm. A suitor, perhaps?"

Kat chuckled, "Of sorts, you could say. He's a nice man I've been seeing. It gets a little lonely here, sometimes. I enjoy his company, nothing more." She fussed with the buttons on her blouse.

"Uh huh." Ivy smiled conspiratorially. "I see. I won't mention it to the others until you're ready to tell them yourself. You just enjoy life, Grandma. It's too darn short."

"Yes, well, I guess I will do just that. Now, where were we again? Oh, the family tree."

"Well, so far, all I know is that you married into the Fox family, and that you are of Ukrainian descent. Kim said you had letters and photos that might be of interest."

"Yes, I do. Let me get my memory box out." She slowly lifted her body up, trying to hide the obvious knee pain she must be having. "Here it is. It's in the old trunk I use as a coffee table." She pulled out a faded, red velvet album and a very old book, as well as a box of pictures.

"Let me get my tablet out so I can take notes," said Ivy, reaching into her tote bag. "Okay, I'm all set."

Grandma Kat sat next to her on the couch and placed her items on top of her antique trunk/coffee table. "I don't have much that will help you, I'm afraid. My mother didn't know a lot about her heritage."

"Well, let's start there. Who are your mother and father?"

"My mother was called Julia, but her real name was spelled Y-u-l-i-a. And her last name was Kuzik. She married my father, Anton Karpenko, in 1932; I was born shortly after in 1933. That's all I know about her, because she never talked about her past. She told me both her and my father were from a long line of gypsies in the Ukraine, but she didn't know much because *her* mother wouldn't talk about it. Gypsies were not well thought of then. In order to fit in, they hid their heritage."

"So when were your parents born? Do you know that?" asked Ivy hopefully.

"Oh, yes. Mother was born in 1900 and Father was born in 1901. I know that because they always teased that she was so much older. They were both born in the United States, but I'm not sure where, somewhere out East; it was my grandparents who were the immigrants; that would be Fox's great-great-grandparents."

Ivy was writing down everything she could, but the older woman was speaking at her usual speed, making it difficult to keep up. "My grandfather was named Petro Karpenko. I'm not sure when or where he was born, but he moved to Walloon Lake in 1913. We only know that because there is a plaque on the property stating the date he purchased the land. He hand-carved a marker into some wood, because he was so proud to be a landowner in America, but after many years it began to deteriorate, so my father made a brass plaque and placed it on a post out by the water's edge."

"Oh, I'll want to see that! I'd loved to take a picture of it for the file."

"You're making a file?"

Ivy laughed at the expression on Grandma Kat's face. "Yes, it's how I work. I need to keep visuals around me whenever possible. Hmm, that means your father was 12 when they moved here. He must have known Ernest Hemingway, too, then. Maybe they played together. Exciting! So, what else do you know?"

"That's it. Like I said, they weren't interested in talking about their childhood. In order to fit into society they had to hide the gypsy connection. And they had too many other problems occupying them, like raising a family and keeping food on the table. People back then didn't dwell on the past. But anyway, maybe some of these things can help you."

Leaning forward, Ivy asked, "What do you have there?"

"These are letters from the Ukraine and an old book, but they're all in the old language, and I can't read any of it. I kept it because my mother said it was important to pass down to the family, but I never understood why. She said she got it from an old gypsy woman named Gina. I don't see the connection. I'm not sure who would want it if you can't read it. But maybe it will be of some interest to you. Kim always intended to do something with it, and then she got too busy raising her family."

At the mention of the name Gina with the word gypsy in the same sentence, Ivy stiffened, but she held her shock in check. It wouldn't do to go down that path at the moment, but she felt the hairs on her arm stand up. Ivy ran her hands over the old letters, which were tied in a bundle with a tattered satin ribbon. The blurry postmarks showed dates in the 1890s. She slowly opened the book which had a leather cover that was cracked and drying. Its parchment pages were thin and delicate and seemed as if they would fall apart at any moment. She turned the papers one by one, careful not to tear anything. She decided it might be a child's book, because there were beautiful illustrations of mountains and flowers. The way the script was set up, in short lines and in a columnar fashion, it looked as if it could even be a poetry book. Ivy's hands trembled. There was something very special, here. She checked the front and back pages to see if there was an inscription. Quite often books of this quality were given as gifts. She was thrilled to find an inscription on a front page that was fading with age, but it could still be deciphered if a person knew the language. It was in a Cyrillic language, the letters and symbols unknown to Ivy. Her excitement was building now. This might be the key to unlocking the family tree.

"Do you have a copy machine? I'd love to make copies so I could study these items at home."

"I do have one but it doesn't work, or maybe it's the operator, but I have had Fox try to work on it before with no luck. Why don't you just take these home with you?"

"Oh, Grandma, you don't want them to go out of the house, do you? I'm not really part of the family tree."

"Of course, you are girl! You are a Marzetti/Fox/Karpenko now. And someday this will be of interest to Sal. And anything you can find out, is way more than we know now. These things don't do anyone any good turning to dust in an old trunk."

Ivy hugged her new grandmother. It felt good to be loved and trusted by an older generation once again.

"I'm home!" said Fox softly, as he peeked in the door. "How are you girls getting along?"

"Perfectly," said Ivy, tears spilling from her eyes. "What took you so long?" she asked, but then she caught the look on her husband's face. He turned his head away, then looked at his shoes, and with a wife's intuition she knew there had been trouble he did not wish to share.

Chapter Eight

Fox kept his eyes downcast. He was sure that Ivy would detect his discomfort and would be able to tell he was hiding something. He had no idea how he would tell her. What was worse was that he wasn't sure how to fix it *without* telling her – or even if he should. Maybe there was a way out. He needed outside advice. It would have to wait until they got home so he could consult an attorney. Why had he never disclosed his secret? Surely she would have been understanding, but now that he had kept it from her for so long, she would be furious. He had seen her rage before, and did not relish being on the brunt end of it again. It could destroy them.

It all started when he had gone to town for the diapers. The universe sure had a way of playing havoc with a person's life. If only Ivy had brought the diapers along. If only he had gone into the gas station/quick stop instead of the grocery store. If only he had chosen another lane. If only, if only, if only. None of it mattered now. He had run into her in the checkout aisle. Why was she even here? Had she followed him? Of course. Piper always knew where he was when she wanted something. She must have run into Sue Anders and quizzed her on his whereabouts. Fox stopped cold in his tracks, when the knowledge hit him that he had been set up. Piper had planted her friend at the house inspection so she could drill him. She knew he had been steering clear of her, and so she had created a 'chance' encounter so she could talk to him once again. How could he have been so stupid, on so many levels? He thought of himself as a fairly intelligent man, but when it came to that woman, nothing ever went his way, and it hadn't since the day he met her.

Fox had been standing in the checkout line choosing a candy bar for Ivy, when a whiff of a very expensive perfume drifted his way. It was her signature scent and he knew it immediately, but before he had a chance to turn around, she came up behind him and wrapped her arms around his waist, then nestled her nose in his neck. "Hi stranger," she said softly.

Fox jumped, and spun around quickly. "What do you think you're doing? This is a public place! I'm a married man."

"Oh, really? Are you sure? You don't act like it."

"What do you mean?" Fox sputtered, getting red in the face.

"I mean, you were flirting quite heavily with me at the mansion, and now I hear that Sue Anders said you did the same with her."

"I never made a move on her, or you! How dare you?"

"Fox, keep your voice down. People are looking."

Fox moved up toward the cash register, placing the diapers on the conveyor. He heard her quick intake of breath, and when he glanced up he saw her face go from a sassy smirk to a pasty pale.

"What are those?" she gasped.

"What do you think? They're diapers."

"A nephew or niece, I assume," she whispered. It seemed as though she had run out of air, and talking had become an effort.

"My son," Fox snarled.

"Your s --- son?" she stuttered.

"That's what I said. Now back off and leave me alone." Fox paid the cashier with his debit card, and began to walk away.

Piper threw her item on the conveyor, and said, "I changed my mind. Sorry." Then she ran after Fox, her high heels clicking on the flooring, as all the locals in their sandals and running shoes turned to look.

"Fox, wait. Wait, please. Please, wait up. We have something to discuss."

Fox stopped dead in his tracks, turned towards her, and said with a disgusted look on his face, "We have nothing to talk about."

"Oh, sweetheart, yes we do, and if you're interested in your marriage and family, you had better take the time to talk to me." She placed her hand on his arm, "Please, Fox, this is serious. No games this time, okay?"

Fox looked at her face, a face he knew so well. But there were times when he had not been able to see through her act. She was very good, so with caution he said, "What is this about?"

"We'll need to go somewhere other than the parking lot, trust me."

"I've never been able to trust you. You know that as well as I do. You have not been straight with me once since the day we met."

With a gentle nod of her head, she agreed to his statement. "Well, yes, but I am a bit older now, although I hate to admit it. And I'm quite successful, so I have nothing to prove to my wealthy family anymore. But I always did love you, in my own way, and you were, and still are, I might add, the sexiest man I have ever known. So there were times I really meant what I said. But this time, you *must* listen. Can we grab some coffee or a Coke?"

"Okay," he said reluctantly, "but this had better be good. And only in a very public place. I'll meet you at the McDonald's up the road."

"No, McDonald's won't do. *Too* public. How about that little coffee shop on Main?"

"All right, but you have ten minutes, and then I'm walking out."

"Thanks, Fox. You won't regret it, I promise. See you in a few."

Even with the promise of some dirt news or whatever she was scheming, Fox noticed she couldn't resist swaying her hips and flipping her hair as she walked away. Fox was embarrassed once again at his reaction to her. 'My God,' he thought, 'she's a gorgeous woman.'

≈

Lying in bed next to his wonderful wife, Fox felt so blessed. Her soft whiffle snore let him know that she was fast asleep, as was his normally rambunctious son. There had been no cuddling with Ivy tonight; she had refused his advances, saying, "Not in Grandma's house." He had needed it more than ever to reaffirm his love for her. He needed to let her know that she was his life and that he couldn't live without her. But left cold with emotions untold and unexpressed, he tossed and turned, thinking over the events that had occurred in the grocery store and later in the coffee shop. His mind wouldn't stop thinking about how he should deal with this, and what the proper words were he should use to minimize the damage. He wondered how judgmental she would be. He had been through that once already with her. He decided the best course was to wait and talk to someone else, an outsider who could offer an objective opinion, but all of his family members were strong Ivy supporters. He most likely needed a legal opinion, anyway, once again.

What Piper had told him had cut him to the quick and shaken him more than he had ever thought possible. First there was shock, then anger, then total disbelief. He had hoped to never see her again in his life, but now it was impossible. They had too much to settle and work out. His head was spinning and pain was stabbing him in the temples and eyes. He got up to take an aspirin, and when he moved she stirred, reaching out for him in her sleep, trusting him. But when she discovered what he had to say, she might never trust him again.

"Fox aren't you interested in this? It's fascinating."

He was a coward, he knew that. But he had decided to tell her when he had all of the facts, good and bad. It wouldn't do any good to let her worry and fret along with him. "What is, my love? What has you so worked up?"

"You know how I've been obsessed with the letters and photos your grandmother gave me."

"Yes, you've practically talked of nothing else. I knew you could be single-minded, but this is crazy."

"I know, but it's so important to me. I'm starting to feel out a story, here. I just need to get back the translation of that book and those letters. I know there's something exciting there, but I had no clue how to get at it. I'm so glad the librarian knew of someone in their genealogy society who could speak and write Ukrainian and other dialects of the area. She said it might take her two months or more, and that time is almost here."

"Two months? It's been that long since we went to Walloon Lake?" asked Fox, incredulously. Where had the time gone, he wondered.

"*Over* two months, silly. It took me time to go over the family tree and then to do some research of my own before I connected with Delia, the translator."

"How much is this going to cost us?" Fox was worried that Ivy was going overboard with this thing. It was just a family tree.

"Oh, Fox, I've told you several times. Don't you ever listen? This is all part of my author account. I'm covering all of the costs connected to this project, since it's for my next book."

"Okay, as long as you don't break *our* bank. Business has been down for me."

"Yes, it's too bad that you lost that account for the mansion. What was the problem?"

Fox hesitated before speaking. He wanted to say this so that there was no suspicion of wrongdoing. "We didn't have a meeting of the minds. Some things are difficult to work out. It was better left alone. Don't worry, I'll find work in other areas." She kissed him and wrapped her arms around him lovingly, as she patted his back gently. He truly did not deserve her.

"Come here and sit with me a moment. This is your family tree. You should be more interested in it than I am. Besides, I have news."

He put on a smile and did what he was told. Anything to please her. He would do anything to please her for the rest of his life.

"Here, look at this chart. Your Grandma Kat told me this much. Here you are, then your mother and father, then we go back to her, Kataryna Karpenko, then her father Anton Karpenko and her mother Yulia. Now it gets really good. Anton's father was Petro Karpenko, born in 1892, Ukraine. I found him in the immigration records and on a ship manifest and passenger list. He came to the US in 1913, and in 1934 he applied for US citizenship and he listed his father as Nikita Karpenko, born 1866, Ukraine."

"Wow, you've really gotten back far." Now he was impressed. His wife was truly amazing. "But it's just a bunch of names."

"For now." said Ivy. "But there's a story here, and I'm going to figure out what it is."

Fox thought of himself. "Not everyone has a story, Ivy."

"Yes, they do. That's the beauty of being an author. You will never really run out of things to write about, if you work at it."

"But aren't you being a little nosy into other people's business, then?"

"Maybe. But these people are long gone. It can't possibly hurt them or anyone they know now. And who knows? Maybe they would have wanted their story to be told."

He kissed her nose. "And you are just the one to do it, my sweetness. Never change. Now go write a bestseller."

"I plan on doing just that! As soon as the translations come back, I'm going to be MIA for a while. Sal will be your job whenever you're home. I'm hoping today the translations will be in my email," she grinned, crossing her fingers.

He loved seeing her excitement. Her whole face was lit up with happiness. Today, he should tell her, but how could he take her down now?

Two days later, Ivy stood anxiously next to the printer, waiting for the documents to print out. Translations of the letters and the book itself had finally come through. She was so excited her fingers were shaking. This was going to be something big – she just knew it!

The determined author read well into the night, long after Sal and Fox had gone to bed. Nighttime was the best for her. She didn't have to worry about being interrupted every few minutes, and it was so quiet that she could get lost in her thoughts. What she discovered was unbelievable, and if she was right, she not only would have a bestseller, but it would change everything for the family.

As she laid out the letters and documents in front of her on the table, she could hardly believe it herself. It looked as if this book had actually been possession of Yulia, Grandma Kat's mother, and Fox's great-grandmother. According to the letters that were sent to her from the Ukraine, her family and the Karpenko family were both part of the same Romani, or gypsy, troupe in the old country. There was one letter that had never been sent. Yulia writes to her husband Anton's family of their marriage, saying she had met Anton in Walloon Lake where his father Petro had settled after immigrating in 1913. Her family had followed the same path, also, to this beautiful part of the country where some of the same flowers and trees grew as they had at home. There were no mountains here, but the terrain was rolling. Lumbering work in the woods was plentiful and there were great places to farm and fish. Life was good, she had said. She apologized for the letter coming from her, but her husband had so far refused to learn to write. She was also sorry if their union caused any distress, because she knew there was bad blood between her family and the Karpenkos. Gina had started it all many years ago, and it seemed her crime might never be forgiven. But it was a new world here, she said. People don't think of gypsy troupes and kings and princes and age-old Eastern European traditions. Along with the new language, she had learned how to love and forgive, and Anton had forgiven her for her family's betrayal. He was handsome and her prince, she said. They had made a pact to never talk of the past, but she had felt it was important to write at least one letter to tell of their marriage. They were so much in love and had already begun to start their own family. She said they were expecting their first child soon. She would be a healing child. Yulia was sure she would be a girl, because girls were gentle and kind. Yulia would teach her to love, not to hate. She would call her Kataryna, named after no one. Someday she would learn the story of how two families, both gypsy, had come together, but for now Yulia begged for harmony as the families were joined with this child.

Ivy was in shock. A woman named Gina, a gypsy woman, was connected to Fox's family through his maternal great-grandmother. Of course, it couldn't possibly be the same Gina she had met at the Frauenthal Theater -- the same old woman who initiated the meeting of Ivy and her fourth cousin Ronnie which led to solving the mystery of Ruby's true father, Max. She could not possibly be the Gina who had first passed on the ruby and diamond necklace to Edward in London. These people were on Ivy's family tree and generations apart. This was crazy! How can any of this be possible? But then, how can a necklace bring lovers together in the magical way it had – Edward and Clara, Maisy and Max, Ruby and Sal. The gems had been lost in the basement at Ruby's cottage, until years later when Fox had discovered them, and as he held them in his hands, they had glowed and vibrated. Ivy knew only too well the power those gems held for her and Fox. She smiled to herself remembering the passionate nights she had spent in the arms of her man with the necklace draped around her throat.

So, somehow, she surmised, Yulia and Anton had met in Michigan, and without the powers of the necklace, had joined together. A fluke? Or a well-laid plan of the universe?

Ivy rubbed her eyes. They were burning with the strain, and she was so tired -- but the book -- she touched the original leather-bound copy. She traced the title with her fingers, and it began to vibrate and hum, much in the same way the necklace had done. She jerked her hand back in surprise, but another part of her had expected it all along. She couldn't resist; she had to start reading just a little bit, so she turned a page of the typed manuscript and read the inscription. In the original copy this part was handwritten and faded to an almost illegible print, but apparently the translator had been able to make it out. It said, 'Protect what is yours.' Then below that was written, 'It is more precious than rubies and diamonds.' Rubies? Does that mean rubies are mentioned in this book of poetry? A mere fairytale? Obviously, there was much more to this story, but if she was to make any sense of it, she would need sleep. Tomorrow night she would stay up late again and read the story she knew she was meant to know.

Anya and Bo – Ukraine, 1868

Chapter Nine

Anya watched every night for the shooting star, but it never came again. Soon it would be time to go back down to the village, and she would have to make a decision about Leonid Palyichak. Marrying the old man might be the only way to save her family's farm, and provide them sustenance and an income in order to live, but she would not think of that today.

She stretched and yawned. What a wonderful way to wake up every morning. The dew had settled on the lilacs early this morning, the dampness sending out the most delicious fragrance. The hills were covered with them, turning the whole mountainside into luscious blends of pinks and lavenders. Birds were calling to each other as they bounced from pine to pine, searching for mates and sharing the discovery of some new seeds with their flock. Anya pulled back the cover from the opening to her small hut. She was so happy her brother had built this protection for her before he died. It was small, very small. It barely fit her and Sasha, but was well-made with branches and twigs tightly laced together and it even had a sheepskin covering on the roof. She preferred to sleep outside but sometimes storms unexpectedly came roaring through – she had been caught in them more than once and had had to huddle under a tree, holding her blanket over her head, knowing that she was in the worse place possible if there was lightning involved. And then she would get drenched to the skin. After the storm had passed and she really needed a fire to warm herself, all of the wood would be wet, so she would have to wait it out until the sun came up and she could dry off. Those times, when it rained for several days in a row, were miserable. After complaining to her father, and stating her case, that if she got sick she would be no good to anyone and might even die out there alone, her father had allowed her brother two small pieces of hide stitched together for the overhead covering. Now she could tuck herself in and still leave the covering pulled back on the dry nights, the better to see the flock in the moonlight.

Anya watched the sheep gently grazing, a nibble here, a nibble there, with only small bleats now and then, so she knew all was well. "Go to sleep, Sasha. You deserve a good rest. I will watch the flock now." The large dog instantly laid down at her feet near the fire she had started as she prepared for the morning meal. He turned in circles until he found just the right spot and sighed deeply as he closed his eyes, knowing he had done his job well all through the dark of the night. But it wasn't more than a few seconds when he raised his head up, fully alert. He stood and looked to the west, a low growl came from his throat. Anya recognized his warning, and grabbed her crossbow. And then she heard it, too. It was the thunder of horses' hooves. She began to quake in fear. Gypsy bands of young rowdy men were known to raid the mountains, sometimes stealing sheep and cattle for their troupe camped nearby, but she had heard of other things they did to young women, and although she wasn't sure of the details, she knew it was bad. So bad that several young girls had been married off in a hurry to local men to protect their reputations.

The horses pounded through the tree line, breaking into the clearing, causing the terrified sheep to scatter. There were three of them, young men in their teens or early twenties, probably out for a morning hunt or scavenge. Their garb told her she was right; they were indeed gypsies. Bells jingled in the horses' manes, and brightly colored scarves were wrapped around their heads. Their tunics were decorated with symbols that were unfamiliar to her. They were most likely from the Hutsuls, or Boykos, traveling tribes that inhabited Galicia, the Western area of Ukraine. There was nothing she could do but to stand her ground. She pulled back the drawstring in preparation for a fight, even though she knew full well who would win this battle. Still, she refused to show fear.

"Bo!" called one man. "Bo, come quickly. Look what I have found." As he approached, his horse walking slowly, Sasha growled loudly, and lowered himself, ready to pounce if necessary. The dog was only waiting for the command from his mistress.

At the call of his name, a young man turned his head, while at the same time his horse spun around.

Even in her fear, Anya could see that he was beautiful. She could find no other word. His tunic was far more decorated than the others. He had some gold coins hanging on chains around his neck, and his sword flashed with jewels. He had a dark complexion, golden bronze almost, as if he were a highly polished statue; perhaps he spent much time in the sun. He wore a long dark braid hanging down his back, with a colorful scarf tied around his head. As he neared she could see the deep brown walnut color of his eyes. They crinkled with unexpected surprise. As the other man lowered his body toward hers, as though he was about to pick her up, the man named Bo called out a command in a language she did not understand, and the other man retreated. Bo walked his horse over to her, and smiled. Then he gracefully slid off his majestic stallion to stand in front of her.

"Pretty Miss, have no fear. We are not the same men as the legends you have heard of. We do not rape women. We do not defile property. May I get down from my horse without being shot?" he laughed.

Anya cautiously lowered her bow, but held it in her hands ready to use if needed. She lifted her chin in defiance. "Are you not here to take from my flock? If it is true, then do so quickly, and go."

"Yes, we might do that. I make no promises. We, too, get hungry. But our people have enough of their own sheep to take care of themselves. We only 'borrow' fruits and vegetables when we are traveling. Do you have any such things to share?"

"No, I do not. Now get off of our land."

"Oh, lovely miss, I know better than you. You do not own this land any more than we do. It is for all the citizens in the area."

"But you are not a citizen!" And she spat at his feet. "You are Tsyhany, lowly travelers, nothing but marauders, pillagers, and thieves." Anya was not even sure where she had gotten the courage to say such things, but they were coming out of her mouth, nonetheless.

His eyes narrowed, and she instantly knew her mistake. He studied her blue eyes and saw tears being held in check. Then he reached out to caress her cheek. Yes, she was lovely, breathtakingly beautiful in fact. She pulled her face away. "Such courage, little one." His hand slowly ran the length of her arm until he reached her hand, then he wrapped his fingers tightly around her wrist. She tugged back, and the dog growled louder. Bo looked at the dog. He could take it down in a second, as could his friends. But he would never harm the girl, and the dog seemed to sense it. He could see its body relax slightly. Bo laughed out loud. "Such bravery. How old are you anyway, little girl?"

Anya tossed her head. "I am *not* a little girl. I am nineteen years old and soon to marry."

"Marry? Then why would your future husband leave you on this mountain all by yourself? What kind of man would do that? That is no man at all! I fear you are not telling me the truth."

"It's no matter what you think. Go on your way and leave me alone. Take a sheep and leave." Her eyes defied him, and now he was very intrigued. He studied her innocent face a moment and dropped her wrist.

The horses of the other two men pranced and sidestepped, eager to be on their way. But the men remained quietly seated, waiting for Bo to make a decision. If he decided to stay with this girl, they would do as he said, and move quietly to the tree line. If he wanted her for himself, they would respect his wishes. He was their prince; they would never repeat anything that happened when they were on their daily rides.

They were there for his protection, but they were also his best friends. Their love for each other had been bonded at childhood, during the crowning ceremony, when they were assigned the prestigious job of being his guards. Bo's older brother had been the prince and heir apparent, but he had been killed in a skirmish with a neighboring troupe, and now Bo would bear the responsibility of caring for the Hutsul troupe one day, when he ascended to Tsyhany King. It was a big job, and for the rest of his life he would have to make crucial decisions pertaining to his people; but along with that came enormous responsibility, so sowing wild oats until that time came was expected and tolerated.

Bo stepped closer so only Anya could hear what he said. "You are a girl of rare courage. I admire that. I want to hear more of this future marriage. I'll be back, little one."

Despite herself, Anya felt a quickening in her pulse. He was a gypsy, a cunning thief and a liar; everyone knew what they were. She could not understand her reaction to him. It frightened her and drew her in at the same time. She watched him mount his horse, and when he glanced back at her, locking her eyes to his own, her knees went weak. Then he turned his shiny black stallion and rode off at a gallop, leaving the space around her empty and void of oxygen.

As the small group crested the hill and disappeared into the tree line, Anya exhaled slowly. "What just happened, Sasha? Why did you not lunge at his throat and protect me? Did you feel it, too? The threat that was not truly there?" The dog knew instantly what his mistress was saying and lowered his head in shame for his lack of aggression. Anya reached out and scratched behind his ears. "It is okay, my friend. We are still alive." Sasha wagged his tail, and took a quick lick of her palm. Once he tasted forgiveness, he turned back to his duties with the flock, leaving Anya alone to contemplate what she would do if the man named Bo returned.

≈

The three horses pounded into the camp, kicking up clods of dirt. An old woman hanging clothes on the line shook her fist at them, calling out swear words, but when Bo blew her a kiss, she laughed. He was wild and crazy but still a favorite with the entire troupe, and would have been even if he had not been the chosen one. His personality was for the most part even-tempered, but at times he had shown a fierce anger when he was protecting one of his own. He truly loved people, so he connected well with both the males and the females, but if you were to ask anyone, they would say it was the females who worshipped him and would do anything he asked. Yet, he never took advantage of that gift.

Bo's dark good looks went well with the bright colors the troupe loved to display around the campsite. They were all artists at heart, seeing beauty in their surroundings everywhere they looked. Scarves of yellows, purples, and oranges hung at the opening to the main tent. The wooden carts some chose to live in were painted with bright red flowers and green trees. A large white tent, was decorated with scenes of the stars and the moon. It was placed close to the communal fire, where the council met to discuss important issues, such as, where to move, and when the best time would be to travel based on when the seer had determined the heavy rains or deep snow would be rolling in. It was important to follow the grasses so the horses, sheep, and cattle could be fed. The need to study nature's cycle was imperative for life. When the salmon were running, they would move close to the streams, and when the deer were at their plumpest, they would move to their favorite forest. Sometimes it was a matter of needing wild medicinal herbs which they collected in the fields, or berries on the bushes when there was a shortage or fruit. Over centuries, the elders had passed on their knowledge on how to take care of themselves, preferring to remain beholding to no man. Freedom was of the utmost importance, and if that meant once in a while they had to help themselves to someone else's apples or corn, then so be it. There was always plenty to go around in another farmer's field, and they were careful to take only what they needed. Survival was the main goal, and tradition was the only way to achieve that goal. Passing stories around the campfire so the young could learn was a weekly happening.

The three young men jumped off their horses and landed gracefully on the soft moss under a large oak tree. A young boy about ten years of age was waiting to take the horses from them. It was his job to help groom the mares and stallions and keep them at the ready in case the men had to ride out quickly. His name was Vasil, and he was more than proud to serve his Prince. "I hope you had a fine ride today, my lord." He took a deep bow from the waist.

"Please, Vasil, do not bow to me. I have not yet taken over the troupe, and I pray my father has a long reign. For now, I am only Bo Karpenko, son of the Tsyhany king of the Hutsuls, Stas Karpenko. Do not promote me too soon. I have too much living to do before the weight of those responsibilities are thrown upon me."

"Yes, Bo. I will do as you wish." Vasil bowed his head and backed away. The men laughed.

"I think he takes his job very seriously, Bo." said Dmytri Lysko, Bo's best friend and trusted guard. "Keep an eye on him though; his loyalty will be useful someday.

Bo slapped Dmytri on the back. "You are right, my friend, but I plan to live my life without reproach, so there will be no need for secrets that need to be kept. My life, unfortunately, is open for all to study. And that is as it should be. Just because I was born into the royal family, does not mean the council will automatically approve me. I must live an exemplary life, as my father has. I must prove I am capable of leading the people to greener pastures every season."

"And you must prove you are capable of continuing the line," laughed Mikhail Kapinos, Bo's other sidekick, as he grabbed his crotch. "That will be the most fun to experiment with."

Bo raised an eyebrow, a trick that usually made the girls swoon. "Mikhail, is that all you ever think of?"

"And why not, when there are so many girls who are willing to help you with your endeavor?"

"I have had my share of trysts in the woods, but I have chosen to be careful. I am not yet ready to become a father.   It is just another one of the many responsibilities which will be thrust upon me. You, my friends, are free to find a girl to warm your bed. One who will make you a good stew and bear your children, but I will have to mate with someone from the group that the council and my father has selected for me; and then when I choose, we will be expected to produce the next heir."

"Ah, such a difficult life," laughed Dmytri. "Trying out all of those lovelies who have been selected. I wish I had your problem."

"Look, I think our people are beginning to form around the fire. It is time to eat, and hear the stories of the day. Promise you won't breathe a word of the girl we found today in the hills. I do not want her being harmed by any of the rowdy men who do not have the same principles as I. They might look at her as fair game since she is not Romani."

The men nodded their heads solemnly. "You have our silence, my lord, as always," they said in unison.

Chapter Ten

Bo tossed and turned all night. It was not like him, as he was usually a very good sleeper. His bedding was tangled up around his legs, the straw was poking him in the buttocks, and he was irritated. And worse yet, was that he could not get the image of the girl in the mountains out of his head. She was so young and innocent, and yet she had a worldliness about her that was very intriguing. He could tell she was smart and cunning. Her eyes were clear blue like the midday sky, and even in her fear, he noticed how she was not afraid to study him. There was a pull between them that he had never felt with any of the girls in the camp. She felt it, too, he could tell. He had wanted to touch her face, stroke her hair, and more. And the worst thing was that he didn't even know her name. What kind of a man didn't take the time to give a girl respect by introducing himself to her? Of course, that would mean admitting that he was a prince, and he wasn't sure he was ready for that, yet. Some women looked at that as a way to gain riches and power within the troupe. The wife of a king had many advantages. He would make it his mission to visit her again, and learn all about her, but he would have to be discreet. If his father found out he was seeing a gadji, a non-Romani, he would be in much trouble and would be brought up before the council. It could jeopardize his ascent to king. He would have to find a way to sneak off in the night, so no one would be the wiser. He had done it before with the help of his two trusted friends; it would happen -- soon he hoped. He would make it happen.

≈

Anya tossed and turned all night. She could not get the handsome stranger out of her mind. She was puzzled why she had had such a reaction to him. After all, he was everything her family hated. The Tsyhany had raided their sheep and cattle for hundreds of years. It was well-known that they were not to be trusted. The villages always breathed a sigh of relief when the travelers moved to another area of the country. Let that village deal with them for a while.

In all the years Anya had been coming up to the mountains with her flock, she had never had an encounter with a Tsyhany. Looking back, she realized that they had not meant any harm, especially the one they called Bo. They were likely planning on teasing her a bit, just to put some fear in her, but she had shown them! She had no fear. Little did they know that she had been quaking inside, even though she knew that Sasha would defend her with his life, if need be.

The crickets and night birds were exceptionally noisy tonight. The air was cool and still and the sky was clear. On such a night, Anya usually preferred to sleep outside, but tonight was different. For all of the bravery she had shown, she had been more frightened than she had admitted to herself. When the sun had dipped below the horizon and the evening turned to black the color of coal, she thought of the close encounter she had had. Perhaps there had been more to fear than she first thought. Sleeping inside was the wisest choice. She would need to depend on Sasha to watch the sheep. He would alert her if anyone approached.

Anya worried through half the night, but soon exhaustion took over and she drifted off to dream of a dark-haired gypsy on a large black stallion, fearful that he would return, but at the same time wanting him to do just that.

"Dmytri," whispered Bo. "Dmytri, over here!" He hissed and gestured from behind a tree.

"What are you doing, hiding like a fox?" asked his friend.

"I don't want Mikhail to see me. I have a request of you, and it is not for his ears."

"It is not like you, my lord, not to include Mikhail in everything we do." Dmytri was puzzled but honored that he had been singled out.

"This is a very special mission, and the fewer who know the better. I need help escaping the camp tonight. No one can know where I am going."

Dmytri slapped his forehead. "Oh, I see it now. You are still thinking of the maid in the mountains. But why not just go with your proper guard? Mikhail would never betray you."

"Yes, of course, I know that. But someone needs to stay behind and tell them that I am safe in my tent, if asked. And you know he is not a good liar. If he knows my intent, then he will surely tell all, if only through his actions."

"You are right," added Dmytri. "Mikhail is better off not knowing; then if asked, he will have the look of truth on his face. What is the plan?"

"You will distract him so I can slip out behind his back, and I will meet you on the other side of the clearing with the horses. Vasil can be trusted. He will ready my stallion and your mare. Can you do this for me?"

139

"Of course, my lord, I am always your humble servant," he bowed in mock servitude and the two shared a good laugh. Then Dmytri winked at Bo at the liaison that was to come. "Are you to leave me alone in the woods, then, while you share a tryst with your peasant girl?"

"I'm sorry, but I have no other choice. I must have a guard at my side at all times. That is a hard and fast rule of the council. No one would think twice that I am leaving in the middle of the night, I have freedom to do as I wish, but I cannot go alone. And of course, if they find out what I was doing in the dark, I would have to face the wrath of the King. I will have to be very careful. I am not to produce a child who will thin the bloodline. Protecting the Boykos and Hutsuls ancestral line is my utmost job."

"I understand. Leave it all to me. I will work it out with Vasil; he will be more than happy to help us."

The two young men walked their horses quietly away from the camp. It had been easier than they thought to slip away. "Just a few more paces and then we can ride, "said Dmytri.

Bo nodded in agreement. "Thank you so much, my friend. I could not have done this without you. The day seemed to drag on with the worry of whether we could pull it off. Mikhail is very sharp. I hope he will not feel betrayed that we have not included him in my escapade."

"I hope it's worth it, Bo. If you are caught, your father will be very angry."

"I'm sure he will be, but I am a grown man. I don't feel the need for a double escort every time I leave camp."

"But you know he is overly protective since your brother lost his life. He needs to be assured that his line will continue in you."

"Maybe so, but I do have a life of my own, and even though I want to be king more than anything, I don't like others telling me what I can and cannot do."

Dmytri laughed. "Spoken like a true king! You have always been a rebel, my brother. I have gotten in more trouble because of you than I would have if left to my own devices. Okay, it's safe to mount our horses now. They cannot hear the pounding hooves from this distance."

The two gypsy men mounted their horses bareback and rode over the hills toward a flock of sheep, a faithful dog, and a young woman who was at that moment contemplating her future with an old man and a farm.

"You know," said Dmytri, "she may not have you. Have you thought of that?"

"Never. Girls cannot resist me. She will be mine." Bo grinned and then winked, but in reality he was not so sure and he would never force her.

In a matter of minutes, they crested the hill and rode into the forest. The path was dark but their horses led the way, following the moonlight they could see on the edge of the clearing. When they came to the opening, Bo requested that Dmytri remain behind.

"She will be fearful, especially when she sees your ugly mug. I must approach cautiously. I think she might be very good with her bow."

"Keep an eye on that dog. I'm sure he will protect her with his life."

"Will you be okay here alone, Dmytri?"

"Of course. I will build a small fire, and I have my bedroll. That's all I need. It is a perfect night to sleep under the stars."

"Wish me luck." He cantered slowly toward her small hut, then slowed to a trot, but he had gone no more than a few feet, when the dog began to fiercely bark and growl. The closer he got the more vicious the sound.

Anya emerged from her hut, worried about what she might be facing. She stood her ground with her bow in hand, fearless as before. When she could detect the black stallion and the man in gypsy garb, she was shaken. Anya wondered why he was here. Did he mean to take her in the way that she had heard whispered of by the women in the village? She would never let that happen. He would have to kill her first. She intended to put up a fight.

He raised his hand in a slight wave and then kept both hands up high, showing he had no weapon. He called out in his language, but she understood that he was saying he came peacefully. She could understand enough of the dialect to know he meant no harm, or so he said.

Bo realized he had spoken in the language of his people, so he converted to a more familiar dialect for her. "Hello, have no fear. I just wanted to talk to you again."

"Why? What could you possibly want from me?"

He could see the fire in her eyes now. She held her head high, her back was straight. She was ready to defend herself if necessary. She had taken out her braids for the night; her hair falling in a long cascade over her shoulder. The moonlight caught her locks giving her an ethereal glow, similar to a halo. She was magnificent.

Bo slowly slid off his horse. "I merely wanted to talk to you again."

"What could you possibly have to say to me? I am only a peasant tending her sheep for her family."

"Ah, but a very beautiful peasant, and I have always loved beautiful women. They are my weakness."

"And you think that flatters me?"

"I'm sorry, I should have not been so bold. I am not used to being rejected." He stepped closer and the dog made a warning lunge. "Would you mind calling off your dog?"

"Sasha, hold." The dog sat closely at her side. "There, but fair warning, he is always on guard. One false move and he will tear out your throat."

"That is good that you have a loyal protector with you. It is dangerous out here. I have been worried for you."

"Ha! I have been taking care of myself for many years now. I have no need for your worry."

"May I come closer? I would love to learn more about you and your culture. I have a thirst for knowledge. It has always been that way since I have been a child. I would like to share with you about my life also, if you care to learn. May I sit by your fire? I would like to warm myself for a bit."

Anya didn't know what to say. He seemed to be moving in like a predator after its prey – like a cat stalking a mouse, slowly and cautiously. But what could be the harm in letting him sit by her fire? She would keep her hand on her bow at all times, just in case. And her knife was tucked into the fold of her garment. She gestured toward the flames which had been dying down to embers, then she reached behind her, into her wood pile and threw on another log. Sparks rose at the contact with the new wood, creating an illuminating light on his face. She felt his sincerity, but was still not sure if she could trust her instincts. They had not failed her in the past, but for some reason her nerves were jangled. She was feeling something new that she had never experienced before. She settled herself on her wool blanket on the opposite side of the fire from the spot he had taken. She tossed him a second blanket to place underneath his britches.

"There, was that so difficult?" he asked. "Now, that we are friends, please tell me your name. I had such bad manners the last time we met. I did not take the time to ask."

"We are not friends, and yes, you had bad manners. My name is Anastasia Pavlovich, but my family calls me Anya."

"Very pretty name, Anya. I am Beauregard Karpenko, Romani prince to the Boykos and Hutsuls, but for you I am simply Bo."

"Ah, so you are a prince. Is that the reason you feel so embolden to approach me the way you have? It means nothing to me. You are not *my* prince."

"That is true, but it is part of my heritage, and I thought you would be interested to know. Will you tell me about your village? About your people? About your farms? I am always gathering information so I can help my people to survive in trying times." He was thrilled that so far she was willing to talk. He loved watching the firelight play off her features. Her face was animated when she spoke, her eyes held no secrets.

"I, too, have always been curious about other people and the way they live. I will tell you my stories if you will tell me yours." Anya realized this might be a dangerous idea, but she also recognized how very lonely she had been. She had been here for many weeks already and there were still many more to come before she could head back down to her village. Contact with this person, especially this very handsome man, was fulfilling a need in her she had not known she had been missing.

This was more than he could have hoped for. She was willing to let him stay for a while. And as it turned out, Anya was a great storyteller. His people would have loved her. She told him about various people in her village in such detail that he felt he knew them. Once she started talking, she did not seem to want to quit. She described what it was like to lose her brother, and to then be asked to marry an old man to save her family's farm.

Bo had a natural ability to tell stories, also. The Tsyhanys, or Romanis, or gypsies, so known by whoever named them, were taught to tell stories from birth. They shared their heritage in this way. He told her about his place in the order of succession and that he, too, had lost a brother, which now made him the prince who was next in line. It was something he had not wanted when he was younger, but now looked forward to. He was eager to show everyone how he could be their leader.

As the two talked, one would throw fuel on the fire while the other was telling about their childhood. When it was Bo's turn to add wood, he would sit a little closer to Anya each time, and she found herself doing the same thing until finally they were side by side like two old friends. They talked way into the night, but when the dawn began to break, Bo knew it was time to go. Anya yawned, and Sasha rose and stretched, now feeling perfectly comfortable with the stranger.

Bo leaned closer still and kissed Anya on the cheek. She looked startled and then smiled. It was her first kiss, and she decided it was quite pleasant. She looked deeply into his eyes as he took her hands in his. They were warm and soft, but at the same time she could feel callouses left from hard labor. They were a strong man's hands, but not an *old* man's hands, as she would soon have to experience when she returned. Bo asked if he could come again the next night, and she thought for only a moment before answering yes. She would let him come back again and again. She would relish the contact with someone she could share stories with, and after she had returned to her family, she would reflect back on these days and remember them for the rest of her life. She prayed it would be enough to get her through, when she was tied down with a man old enough to be her grandfather.

Chapter Eleven

"How was it? Was she all you had hoped for?" Dmytri was eager to hear all about Bo's escapade.

"It was what I had expected and nothing more." For the first time Bo was not willing to share anything about his time spent with Anya. "She is a very unusual girl," he said, "and that's all I'm going to say."

"Oh ho! She must have been something special, then. Will you give permission to Mikhail and myself to share in your pleasures?"

"Never! Stay away from her. If you go anywhere near her, I will kill you!" Bo was surprised at his own outburst. He had never raised his voice at his good friend in anger.

Dmytri sucked in his breath at hearing Bo's passion. "I am so sorry, my friend. I had no idea she meant so much to you. You were only with her a few hours. Was she that good?"

Bo lunged at Dmytri across their horses' bodies and dragged him to the ground. He began to pummel Dmytri's face and body. His anger had taken him to another place outside his own body. From far away he heard his name being called.

"Bo, Bo, stop. I cannot return your blows. Stop. You know I am not allowed to strike back. Bo!" he grunted.

With his rage dissipating somewhat, Bo began to focus on Dmytri's words. Yes, it was not right that he was the only one fighting. Dmytri would take anything he gave him, and never raise a hand to defend himself. Bo had never done anything like that before, and he was ashamed. He pulled himself off of his loyal friend and stretched out a hand to help him up. "I am sorry and embarrassed that I struck you. Am I forgiven?"

"Of course, you are. I was out of line to suggest I could share in your conquest. I, too, am embarrassed."

The men got back on their horses and began a slow walk while they talked. "You see, she was not what I expected. She is sweet and intelligent and oh so innocent. She is beautiful and kind and she is loyal to her family. She is everything a prince looks for in a wife."

"But she is not Tsyhany, my lord; she is gadji. It can never be."

"But that will not stop me from seeing her. We need to make arrangements so I can have other visits. She will leave the mountain soon; I cannot go into her village to meet her. It is too risky."

"Then the only way is to bring Mikhail into it so he can help, also. We can't continue to do this without him."

"No, the only way is for me to do it alone. I am perfectly capable of taking care of myself, and then you won't have to be implicated in my transgressions."

"I cannot let you do it, my lord!"

"But you must. I command it. Now, it is getting light, let us ride faster so we can be back at camp soon and no one will be the wiser."

And no one was. They returned just before light, and when the two were found tending to their horses with the help of Vasil, it looked as if they were preparing to ride out instead of just coming home. Bo flipped him a gold coin, and the boy grinned. He had never been allowed to hold a coin of that worth before. He was so proud that he pledged his undying loyalty to his prince.

"Now, let us have a meeting with Mikhail and fill him in." Bo was feeling more and more like a king as he barked orders to his guards and explained how he expected that they would not breathe a word. Once they had agreed to cover for him when he was gone, he began to leave camp at regular intervals whenever he could safely get away. Sometimes it was at night and sometimes during the day, because at this point he knew he could not stay away from Anya without his heart breaking in two.

≈

Anya spent more time watching the horizon for Bo's horse than she did watching the sheep. He came back again and again, and soon they became of one heart. During the day they would walk and pick wildflowers, and then return to share their lunch. They always stayed close to the perimeter of the flock; Anya refused to shirk her duties there. But the best time was when Bo came at night. One time when Bo felt she was ready, they spread their blankets on the dewy grass, and laid back, staring at the stars. They talked about life in other cultures and Bo told her about his travels. He told her about other traditions and foods, and through him Anya saw the world. As they lay side by side, on occasion Bo would roll over and kiss her, now on the mouth. They were no longer the quick pecks he had started out with. They were soft and lingering, and then after a time more firm, as Anya pressed her body against his, sometimes arching her back to meet him. She was shocked at her own behavior, but she knew this was all she wanted in the whole world. The layers of clothing each wore prevented much else from happening, but as the summer came upon them and the days and nights were warmer, their lighter-weight clothing was thinner. Anya could feel Bo's firmness against her softness, and she never wanted him to stop caressing her. On one such night, when they lay looking at the stars which had never been brighter, it was exceptionally hot and still; the only fires were a few small ones built closer to the flock to keep predators away.

"Bo, what is to come of us? Soon I will have to go down the mountain, and I am sure my father will insist on my marriage. I have been able to put him off this long, but I am not getting any younger. He knows if I delay the wealthy farmer might change his mind." Anya began to cry at the thought.

"Little one," he soothed, "I will not let anything happen to you like that."

"But how can you prevent it? We are from two different worlds. It is impossible."

"Nothing is impossible. Let's watch the stars and forget about the future for a while. We can ask the universe to help us."

"I am Catholic, Bo. I will pray to God. Here, hold my hand." As she said her prayer to the heavens asking for an answer to their dilemma, a silent tear escaped and ran down her cheek. Bo kissed it away, and all the while his heart was aching. Without knowing why, he prayed to her God, and asked, "Please, Oh Heavenly One, is there a way to be together? Can I convince my father?"

As they stared at the sky hoping for an answer, there was nothing but blackness and twinkling stars. They were so disappointed. "I fear your God does not approve of me."

"That is not it at all! Perhaps it was not yet the time for an answer. We must keep trying."

For the first time, because of the heat, Anya had worn a blouse which exposed her arms. When Bo kissed her, he could touched her flesh. He ran his hands up and down taking in every curve. The contact after all of this time, sent shivers running between them. The kisses were longer, and he became more demanding. Bo moved his body over her peasant dress and leggings, while she strained to join him. He began to raise her skirt, but when he realized what he was doing, he pulled himself back. "We cannot. You must remain a virgin, or your family will know when you marry your farmer that you have been with a man. I have too much respect for you to send you back a defiled woman."

Anya didn't know why but she began to cry, except that she had wanted whatever it was so badly and now the space between them felt empty. Her arms ached for him. She needed him. But Bo rose and said goodbye, leaving her alone and cold. He promised to return soon, and he did -- the very next night. He could no more stay away from her than cut off his sword-wielding arm.

After much thought, Bo had an idea. He now knew his next step, and it was a bold one. The following day he walked with his two guards as they talked in low voices. "I have a plan, but it must be executed perfectly in order to work."

"What is it, Bo?" asked Dmytri.

"Anything for you," said Mikhail.

"Yes, anything," agreed Dmytri.

"I need to get something from my father's tent, so I'll need a distraction long enough for me to look around. I'm not sure where it's kept. And then after that I will need an even bigger favor if that works out."

"Of course, what is the plan?" Always ready for an adventure, the two friends listened eagerly to what Bo was asking of them, and agreed to not tell a soul. But when they heard what the follow-up plan was, they objected and tried to talk him out of it.

"It must be. It is the only way I will be happy."

The first part of the plan was that they would get into a rip-roaring fight over a girl. They would fight over Gina who was always eager to go with a man. That would bring out the entire troupe who would encourage them with their calls. The gypsies loved rowdiness and as long as it didn't get out of control, any fight was considered a good time. His father would be called to put a halt to it, and that would give Bo enough time to search the tent. He would be looking for something most of the troupe had only heard talk of and considered to be a rumor. It was private and kept only for the royal family, specifically the king and his betrothed, who would then become queen, until it was passed down to a son who was about to marry. Bo had seen it only once or twice, and when he questioned his father about it, King Stas told him not to worry, his time was coming, and to be patient. If he chose the right woman to be his wife, he would be handed it to give to her. The rewards would be great, he had promised, with a wink. It was all he knew about it except its beauty was beyond belief. Bo knew what he was doing was a huge violation, but he didn't care. His love for Anya was so strong it had gone beyond all reason.

The ploy worked. He snuck into the tent the moment both his mother and father left to see what the commotion was. He had only a few moments to look into the ornately carved box sitting next to the bed, which he knew held certain treasures. He pulled out a velvet drawstring bag and withdrew the most magnificent ruby and diamond necklace he had ever seen. He had no idea where it had come from or how long it had been in the family, he only knew it was to be used by direct line descendants. His father said it was meant to keep the line pure. He had no idea how a necklace could do that, but he wanted to show it to Anya. He knew he couldn't give it to her; but for some reason he wanted to share his family's treasure with her. The moment his hands touched the jewels, the necklace began to hum and vibrate. He almost dropped it in alarm, but then he heard voices approaching so he quickly placed it in his inside shirt pocket and stepped out before anyone knew he had been there. Tonight he would show the jewels to Anya, and maybe she would wear it for him. He couldn't wait to see the look on her face.

≈

When Bo saw the bruised faces of his friends, he apologized over and over. They had been so loyal even though he knew they truly did not approve of his growing attachment to Anya. They had both warned him about falling in love, because he was meant to be their king. Nothing good could ever come of this match, they said. Bo argued that he could handle his father's wrath if it came to that, but he had no intention of giving up Anya. So once again he slipped away on his own, and even his friends did not know that he carried a precious necklace in his pocket. He had also placed his favorite sopilka in his satchel. He wished to woo her with the dulcet tones of the highly carved fife. He would surprise her with his singing voice, which he had been told was very pleasant to listen to.

She was waiting for him as he had hoped. The moonlight only added to her beauty as she stood silently next to her dog. Her arms were extended as she eagerly awaited to hold him close to her body. This time when they greeted, they were both surprised with the passion of their kisses. The necklace spread a warmth through Bo's shirt and went straight to Anya's heart. Anya surprised herself with soft moans, as her pulse quickened and her veins seemed to race with hot molten lava. They instantly dropped to the blankets she had placed on the ground near the fire in anticipation of his arrival. Their bodies were eager for each other, but Bo pulled himself back so as to be sure he was not forcing her into anything she did not want to do. Her eyes conveyed her desire for him, and he was pleased.

"Anya, I have brought you a gift. But it is one that I must return after tonight, so you cannot keep it. I wanted to show you a treasure that belongs to my family." He reached into his shirt and withdrew the velvet bag. His hand was already warming, and as he held it, it vibrated more than ever before. When he removed it from the pouch, Anya's eyes opened wide with astonishment. Five large glowing rubies were surrounded by diamonds; it was truly a treasure meant for a queen.

"I want you to wear it for this evening."

Her hands shook as she reached out to touch the jewels. "I have never seen anything like it. I think I am not worthy to place it on my neck. It is for royalty."

"And in fact, you are right; it is for royalty – Tsyhany royalty. This necklace is always passed down from father to son and is meant to be given to the woman who will become his wife, before it is passed to

161

the next generation. I have no idea how many generations my family has owned it, but it has always been ours for as long as the stories go back. Will you wear it for me? I would love to see you dance to my sopilka."

"I am embarrassed to dance for you, but if that is what you want, I will try." Bo kissed her again; his anticipation was growing and he could hardly contain himself, so he placed the jewels around her neck. The moment they made contact with her skin, she became a different person. She was no longer an innocent child. She was a woman of the world who wanted to please her man. At that moment, she knew with every fiber that she could not go back to the old man in her village without first experiencing true love – the love and passion of a virile young man who cherished her and thought she was beautiful. Bo raised the sopilka to his lips and played ancient gypsy love songs that had been taught to him from childhood. He started out slowly, so Anya raised herself up to move around the fire to his notes. Then as the songs began to become more exotic and frantic, she raised up her skirts and laughed for joy at the freedom she felt. She was seductive with her gestures and completely uninhibited. Bo's eyes followed her every move, until finally he could hold himself back no longer. He dropped the fife and danced under the stars with her as he sang the melodies instead. They raised their hands above their heads and clapped the rhythm as they swayed.

Suddenly a large shooting star crossed the sky, and when they stopped to watch as it quickly burned out, the warm tingles in their bodies increased. As they dropped to the blankets and consummated their love, the universe sent one shooting star after another. The sky was ablaze with them. Once the lovers were spent, they lay on their backs and watched the heavenly display go on for hours. After a time of rest, they continued with their lovemaking well into the night.

"Anya, my sweet one, I love you more than life," confessed Bo, surprised that he had spoken these words out loud. He had never said them to anyone else before.

"Oh, Bo, I love you too. What does that mean for us?" cried Anya.

"Let us worry about it tomorrow," whispered Bo, "the night is short and I need you once again."

In the morning, when Bo realized he had spent the entire night with Anya, the reality of what they had done became clear. It was a dilemma he was afraid to face.

How could they possibly be together? She was a peasant and he was a prince. Anya, too, was thinking, that it was an impossible situation. Her family would never accept a Tsyhany, a gypsy, as her husband. She would be disowned, and if they learned of their lovemaking she could be shunned.

When Bo rose to go home, Anya grabbed his hand. "Bo, what will we do now? How will we ever be together?"

"I will think of something; don't worry. I will come back to you tonight with a plan. You are my breath; you are my heart; you are my life. I cannot live without you, and I will not." After several more kisses they finally tore themselves apart, and Bo rode off at a full gallop. He was already terribly late for sneaking back into camp, so he was surprised when he met his guards just on the edge of the forest.

"What are you doing here? Spying on me?" he called out angrily.

"No, my lord. When we saw the lateness of the hour, we decided to help you with an alibi. We have killed three rabbits and five partridges. We will go back to camp with you as if we had left together early this morning. They are always thrilled to see fresh meat. No one will think anything of it."

"I apologize for my sharpness. You are so loyal, and my best friends in the world. I must find a way to reward you." Behind his back Dmytri and Mikhail glanced at each other, knowing their prince was in a terrible spot. He had fallen deeply in love with a woman he could not have.

Chapter Twelve

The campground was already bustling with morning activities. Fires had been fed in several locations in anticipation of preparing for the morning meal. The crackling wood caused sparks to fly upward creating a fairyland of light. As the young men rode in with the rabbits at their side, they were greeted with smiles and nods. The small boys stopped their play to admire the prince and his entourage. Vasil was waiting to take their horses. He winked and then blushed at his own impertinence. Bo ruffled his hair and laughed. It was all the acknowledgement he needed from the man he so adored. Bo's mother, Olnya, called out, "There you are, my son. I was wondering when you would show up. But now I have no complaints, because I see you have brought us enough meat for a feast. You are such good boys." She kissed her son and took the meat to the woman whose job it was to feed the troupe. She was more than proud of her handsome Beauregard. No mother could ask for more.

"You see, my prince," whispered Dmytri, "all it takes is a good hunt, and you will be forgiven anything."

"Thank you again, my friends. But now I have to figure out how to return the item I took from my father's treasure box. It is too dangerous to keep for long."

"You can slip in his quarters when everyone is eating. They will think you have gone to relieve yourself in the trees."

"Okay, but keep an eye out, and if someone comes looking for me, cause another distraction."

"Yes, my lord."

Night after night Bo returned to Anya with the necklace in his pocket. Each time he stole the necklace and then returned it to its proper place the next morning, and even though it was becoming more dangerous, it was well worth the risk, because soon they were so free with each other that they dance naked by

167

the fire, the jewels dancing as well, while they made love openly on the ground, and when the mountain storms came upon them, they snuggled under the sheepskin blankets in Anya's little hut as the rubies sparkled and glowed. At first Anya was embarrassed at her behavior, but after a while she no longer cared. She felt such joy to be so free with her lover, and the impulses from the necklace made them forget all shyness. It was like a drug they could not get enough of. They vowed to be together for the rest of their lives, even though they knew that all too soon they would be forced to break their promises.

The men continued to cover for Bo, but they worried daily that it would all come to a tragic end. Little did the men know that one of the young women who was on the list of favorites to be chosen as a bride for Bo had been watching his movements as he went in and out of the gypsy camp. Her name was Gina. She had been trying to find his likes and dislikes so as to have an advantage with the competition when the time came for the selection of his bride. In an attempt to gain Bo's attention, she lowered the neckline of her blouse and raised the hemline of her skirt. She always wore flowers in her hair to add to its cascading ebony beauty.

Of all the women, Gina was the most aggressive but she was also the most beautiful. She had been told so since she was a child, and therefore she was not afraid to use it to her advantage. She had creamy skin and flashing eyes with a large pouty mouth that all men seemed to find attractive. The men did not hesitate to call out suggestive words to her, but it did not insult her; instead, she returned their looks with inviting smiles and shrugs of her bare shoulders. But like her mother and her grandmother before her, she had one more trick she could use. Gina had the ability to see things in the future. And even though some thought that all Tsyhanys, or Romanis, had this ability, they did not. It was, in fact, rare. Many proclaimed to be able to read minds, but it was all a game so as to easily take a gadji's money. Gina knew her abilities were real when she had a vision of her father's passing before he actually died. She was just a child then and thought people would laugh if she mentioned it to anyone, so she kept it to herself. She saw her father falling off a cliff which seemed improbable, because at that time they were living in the valley. But a few months later he rode out to go on a hunt, and while on one of the foothills, his mare lost her footing along a narrow trail and the two went down a large drop-off together. The guilt Gina felt was overwhelming because she had failed to warn him, so she confessed her abilities to her mother, and she was told how to handle them and what to do with them.

Gina was not sure if Bo would choose her or not. That was one thing she could not see, but in her vision she did see him in great trouble, so she thought if she kept an eye on him and she would be able to prevent a catastrophe, he would reward her by making her his wife. She would like nothing better than being queen someday.

So when Gina saw Bo leave the campfire after one of his early morning outings, she followed. She first went in her own direction and then circled back to his path. It was soon apparent that he was heading to his father's tent. Once he was inside she peeked in, hoping he was about to change his clothes. Maybe she could catch a glimpse of his fine frame. She had seen him bathing once before, and was very pleased with the body he had to offer a mate. But instead of a naked body, she saw Bo opening a carved box next to the bed. He retrieved a jewel from his shirt that flashed even in the dim light of the tent. She sucked in her breath, and then placed a hand over her mouth so he would not detect her breathing. She saw rubies and diamonds for just a moment before he placed it in the treasure box; she withdrew immediately because she could tell he was about to leave. She ran into the cover of a nearby bush and waited until he was gone before she came out, and then she thought over what she had just seen. It could mean only one thing. The legend of the necklace was real, and Bo was using it on someone. Her heart sank when she realized he must have already made a choice for a wife and she was not the one.

After all of the months spent trying to gain his attention, Gina still had not progressed beyond a passing glance. Who was this woman who had captured his heart? And what was she to do about it? She could reveal her suspicions to his father, but then if she was wrong, Bo would hate her forever. She sat very still, purposely trying to call up the future. When she was given a vision of a naked Bo and a young women lying in the grass she called out, 'No!' She shook her head to clear the image. She did not want to see it. They had already committed themselves to each other. She knew in that flash that it was over for her.

A rage came over her that turned her vision red. Bo was hers! No one else would be able to please him the way she could. She would see to it that no one else ever tried again. She looked around to see if anyone was near, and when she was confident that she was alone, she did the unthinkable. She crept into the king's tent and stole the necklace. She would hide it where it would never be found. Now if he selected someone other than her, he would not receive the passionate pleasure he was expecting. Maybe he would even have a loveless marriage. The best result would be if he had a childless marriage, because then he would be allowed to take a second wife, and she would make sure it was herself. Gina decided she would hide the gems on her body until he was so obsessed with her that he could not resist her charms.

But the moment she took the necklace and left the tent, she felt a chill, and then remorse for what she had done. She panicked. This thing must be returned. She could be banished from the troupe if what she had done was discovered. No one had ever entered the king's tent without his permission. But the people were moving around. It was time to get on with the daily chores. The women were cleaning up the eating area while the older men returned to their tents to have a smoke and private conversations. It would be impossible to return the necklace now. There was too much activity. She would have to find another time and pray that it was not discovered as missing until she had the chance to put it back. The best solution would be to wear it under her frock. Perhaps Bo would find her to be Irresistible and her worries would be for nothing.

Gina decided until that time came she would stay close to Bo and make sure nothing happened to him. It would be difficult with his guards around all the time, but she was a good flirt. She had learned how to be sexual from her mother. They practiced her side glances and her hip-swaying walk all the time. Maybe she could get close to one of the men and she could convince them to take her on their outings. If she had to, she would give herself to either Dmytri or Mikhail in order to achieve her goal, but she would never allow them to go all the way. She must remain pure for the one she loved. It would not be too bad of a chore -- they were both very good looking Tsyhanys -- and in the doing so, she might be able to glean Bo's secret. She would keep the necklace after all, she decided. It would be her treasure now, and soon he would belong to her. With the heavy jewels around her neck giving her confidence, she was positive she could make it happen.

≈

The next time Bo went into his father's tent to take the necklace, he was shocked to find that it was not in its proper place. At first he went into a panic. He knew he had replaced it just like he had all the other times. He poked around the box and the floor, until he was convinced that it was truly missing. Now what? How could he tell his father what he had done? It was a cherished possession; it had been in their family for generations, and now it was gone and all his fault. Then he smiled to himself. Of course! His father must have removed it himself. He was still a virile man, and very much in love with his wife. His father must have had plans to share the pleasures with Bo's mother, or perhaps he even had a young girl on the side waiting for him in her tent. It was not out of the question. Ha! If that was the case, the king would not bring up the missing gems, because then Bo's mother would know that he had lain with another woman. There would be enough screaming and clawing to be heard in the neighboring hills. Tonight Bo and Anya would be on their own, without the enticement of the rubies and diamonds, but Bo was sure it would not matter at all. They were wildly in love and nothing could interfere with their passion.

When Bo snuck out again that night, Gina was close behind. At times she lost him because it was difficult to keep up since she was on foot, but she could tell the general direction and she followed the well-worn path through the trees. She watched as Bo greeted a peasant girl, and her eyes narrowed as they began to kiss and sway. After the fire was stoked, they tumbled to the earth in sweet ecstasy. The flames cast an orange glow about their bodies as they loved each other in a gentle fashion, slowly as though they were savoring each touch. Gina knew then this was far more serious than a tryst. With tears in her eyes, she slowly walked back to her people. In the morning she would find a way to return the necklace without being noticed. It was over. She was sure of it now. Bo would never love her like he did that girl.

Not having the necklace was the best thing that could have happened for Bo and Anya. That night their love making was sweet and pure. It was like the first time all over again, and when they had finished coupling, Bo was certain he could not live without her.

"Anya, I must have you by my side for the rest of my life. Will you marry me?"

Anya's eyes filled with tears. "Bo, you know I would love nothing better, but we can never be together. You are Tsyhany, and I am a sheep herder's daughter. I've known for a while that our time is running out. When the moon is full, my nephew Vlad, will arrive to take over my duties. We only have a few days left. I am to return to my family and then I am sure my father will insist on my marriage, in order to ensure my family's future by joining our land with Leonid Palyichak's."

Bo's face turned red with anger. "I will *never* let that happen! No one will touch you but me. You are mine, little one. Can't you see? Even without the necklace, we made beautiful love. It can never be duplicated with anyone else, I am sure of it. You are my life and my soul. We have merged together and now we are one. I will not allow us to be separated – ever!"

"But how could that ever work, Bo? Not only would my family be against our union, but yours would be, as well. You are royalty and you represent all the Hutsuls of the region."

"I do not want to be prince any longer. Without you it is meaningless."

"I cannot be the reason you give up your high position."

"Would you rather be with me or your old man with wrinkles and bad teeth?"

Anya laughed. "How do you know he looks like that? You have never seen him."

"Does he not?"

"Well, yes he does have bad teeth, and his breath is like a pig's pit."

"There. You see? I will remove you from the threat of having to spend your life with a pig's pit."

Anya snuggled in Bo's arms. She loved to hear him talk when he was so protective of her, but she still did not see how their union would work. She sighed and then began to sob. "It's hopeless."

"Nothing is hopeless," declared Bo. "I will give up my crown for you. We will run away and be together always."

"But Bo," Anya cried, "what of my family? How will they survive without me marrying Leonid?"

"What if they had never had a daughter? They would have found a way to work it out. It is not up to you to save your family. That is your father's problem. They have sheep to barter, and they can sell both the wool and the meat. They will be just fine."

Anya began to feel a glimmer of hope. "Perhaps you are right. But how would we do this thing you are talking about, and where will we go?"

"I will make a plan and my guards will help me. They are loyal to the end."

"Even if it means they will be losing their prince?"

"Even then," nodded Bo.

"If you are to do such a daring thing, it must be quickly. My nephew will be back when the moon is full, and that is but a few days away."

"Perfect. That way when we leave the sheep won't be alone for too long."

"What about Sasha?"

"You will have to leave him behind to protect the flock, I'm afraid."

"It will hurt to say goodbye to my friend, but it's the least I can do for my father. Sasha will take good care of them until Vlad comes."

"I must go and prepare the plan. I will be back tomorrow night, so be ready to leave."

"So soon?"

"Yes, if we are to make this work it must be then."

"Oh, my love," said Anya, "I look forward to spending my life with you. You have saved this poor peasant girl from a life I could not bear to think about. I love you more than the stars that shine, and more than the earth the moves beneath us when we are joined."

They could barely stand to separate that night, but the promise of a lifetime together motivated them to go their separate ways. They kissed faces and hands and stroked each other's hair, and with tears accompanied by smiles, they finally said goodbye.

When Bo confided in Dmytri and Mikhail what he had planned, they both stated they were firmly against it. They could not help a prince to leave his people behind, but once he described for them the depth of his love for Anya, they began to see that there was no changing his mind. So together they worked out the details of the night to come.

It was decided that they would say they were taking one of the wagons to sell some wares to a village nearby. They had accumulated a mixture of wood carvings and dyed scarves and finely honed knives. It was time to get some cash for the troupe instead of just food supplies. Bo's father agreed but cautioned them because the local people were not always friendly. The young men said they would be back in three days.

Once more Bo took a chance and went into his parents' tent. When he looked for the necklace he was thrilled to see that it was back in its rightful place. So at least he could leave without the guilt of thievery on his conscious.

The men left early in the morning when the dew was fresh on the ground. The dampness rose from the forest floor and created a fog that was mystical and eerie at the same time. It surrounded them with a heavy mist as the wagon creaked and swayed on the path toward Anya, enclosing them like a blanket as they passed through.

She was waiting for them next to her dog. When Bo approached to help her up, she whispered, "Are you sure?"

"I am absolutely sure. I cannot live without you."

Anya hugged her dog's neck tightly. "Take care of the sheep, Sasha. Vlad will be here soon. I wish you could talk to tell him about my journey, so he would know I am safe and happy. You have been a great defender and protector. Thank you, old boy." Anya got into the back of the wagon where Mikhail had placed a heavy blanket, ready to cover her if need be. With tears in her eyes, Anya watched as the landscape passed by. Knowing she might never see these beloved mountains again which were now covered with bright yellow wildflowers, or smell the heavenly scent of lilacs in spring, or watch a fawn walking quietly next to its mother, she prayed for her own safety for she had no idea where Bo was taking her. She also prayed for her family. She asked God to give them peace, for when they discovered she was missing, they would assume the worst.

The wagon moved at a steady pace. There was no need to rush at this point because it was expected that they would be going to the village, and if they were seen, it should look exactly like that. Once past the village, they began to pick up their speed. They would travel south through the Ukraine to Odesa, where they would take a ship on the Black Sea and from there they could work their way toward the Mediterranean. That was the extent of Bo's knowledge of geography, so he could tell Anya no more. But he was sure he could get to Europe somehow after that. Mikhail and Dmytri would go with them, so no one from his troupe would ever be able to track them. That was *their* plan, but life had other happenings in the works.

Chapter Thirteen

The dirt road was uneven, roughly jarring Anya and Bo, who were riding in the back of the wagon. Dmytri and Mikhail took turns driving, calling softly to the horse as they went. Their pace was quick and steady but not rushed. A few people waved as they passed, intrigued by the highly decorated gypsy wagon. Dmytri got out his drymba, a type of Jews harp, and after a time Bo joined the music with the sopilka he had played for Anya many times before. Mikhail sang along to songs Anya had never heard of before, some lively and quick, while others were songs of unrequited love played in a mournful minor key. When Dmytri took the reins,

Mikhail played his balalaika, a triangular guitar. She enjoyed listening to the men who had obviously made music together before. From that time on, it was an idyllic trip, with dreams of the future discussed openly. When the men had exhausted themselves with song, Anya asked, "What will you do, Dmytri and Mikhail? Will you stay with us and form a new life?"

"For a time, I will," answered Mikhail. "But I am looking for a wife. It is time that I settle down and start a family. When it is safe and you are on a ship, I will go back to the troupe."

"How will you explain us?" she questioned.

"We will not mention you, of course. And at first I am sure no one will believe me, but I will say that Bo was robbed at a marketplace, and that we fought back with everything we had, but we were unsuccessful and he died, along with Dmytri. I will say I was not able to bring their bodies back."

"So, Dmytri, you will stay with us?"

"Yes, I will never leave my prince. He is my best friend, and I have pledged to defend him to my death."

"That is comforting," replied Anya.

Bo laughed, "What? Do you not think I am capable of taking care of you?"

184

"Of course, you are, my love. I just meant it is better to have another as a lookout while we are -- um -- sleeping." She blushed such a bright color that the others laughed loudly at her, making her discomfort all the worse.

Finally, after days of travel they arrived in Odesa. It was a busy port town. Anya had never seen anything like it, but the Tsyhany gypsies were well-traveled, and it was nothing new to them. After inquiring about tickets on the next ship, they were disappointed to discover that one had just left port. They were told they would have to wait a week for the next departure. They parked their wagon on the edge of town and made camp. Bo and Anya slept inside, while the two friends slept where they were most comfortable -- on the ground. The couple's lovemaking was quieter than normal, especially without the necklace, but still soft moans could be heard through the wooden structure, and the guards chuckled and made jokes amongst themselves.

The days of waiting were some of the best in Anya's life. They spent their free time roaming through the marketplace, looking over handcrafted items Anya had never seen before. She dreamed of the day she would have a home with Bo and they could shop together; he would search for the proper tools or barter for some grain, and she would select the best cuts of meats and vegetables for their evening meal. Maybe someday they would have a farm of their own and raise items to bring to market to sell. And perhaps children would arrive later and they would help with the harvests. But she knew one thing – she would never force her daughter to marry someone she did not love, no matter what their financial situation was.

One evening when the small group of four were talking around their fire, they heard a rustling in the woods. Mikhail grabbed his knife from his belt, and Dmytri pulled his sword from its scabbard.

Five large men stepped out from the bushes, surrounding them in a threatening way. One called, "Bo, your father sent us to retrieve you." They recognized the men as the King's guard. Dmytri and Mikhail placed their bodies in front and behind Bo to protect him from his own people.

"I am not going back," yelled Bo. "Tell Father, I do not wish to be king. I am going to marry the woman I wish even though she is gadji. I know Father will never allow it, so I am leaving for good."

"You cannot go, my prince," said one of the large men. "We have promised to bring you back, and we will do so -- without the woman." Dmytri made a move toward Anya, and that caused the scuffle to begin. The men were trying not to harm Bo, but they did not care about his guards. In their opinion, his guards had betrayed their troupe. Mikhail received a blow to the head, which rendered him unconscious.

Bo was pinned down on the ground so Dmytri came to his defense, but Bo yelled, "Protect Anya, I command you. Stay with her. Protect her." As the gypsies dragged off Bo and Mikhail, Dmytri pulled a screaming Anya into the dark forest and did as his master asked.

"I will find you, Anya. I will find you, I promise. A-n-y-a!" he called. And then there was a muffled sound and his voice could be heard no more.

When they were alone, Dmytri held Anya with his arms wrapped around hers, as she sobbed for her stolen lover and struggled to follow. "What will we do now?" she cried.

"I will do what was asked of me. I know Bo's plan and they do not, so we will board the ship when it comes in tomorrow, and work our way to Europe. He wanted to show you London, so we will go there and stay for a while, until he can find us."

"Europe? It is so far away. How will he know where to look?"

"Never fear. He has good instincts, and he knows how to ask the right questions. He will find us, but it may take a while. And I have a secret way of communicating with him. It was planned a long time ago, in case of an attack by a neighboring tribe."

"Thank you, Dmytri, for keeping me safe. You are a good man." She collapsed to the ground, sobbing until she fell asleep in his arms. Dmytri understood why Bo had fallen in love with Anya. She was not only beautiful, but kind and compassionate. He would have loved her himself if his prince had not claimed her as his own. So now he would do as he was asked and dedicate his life to hers, as he had to Bo's.

≈

When the men arrived back at their camp, they delivered Bo to his father. The King was furious that Bo had caused so much trouble. He lectured Bo, telling him that he had to obey because he was the last hope for the family, since his brother had passed away; otherwise, the troupe could hold a vote and the line of succession would go to another family. It was his duty to the Karpenkos. His mother pleaded with him to stay with them and fulfill his obligation. "She's not worth it," she said. "There will be other girls. In fact, Gina has expressed her desire for you already," said Olnya. "Is she not beautiful enough for you?"

"Mother, Anya, is my life. I do not want Gina."

"But Bo, Gina has special powers. It was she who told us where you were. She had a vision, and she shared it with us, so we would not lose our prince and beloved son. You would make a great team together."

"No, Mother and Father, you do not understand. I stole the necklace from your treasure box."

"You what?" they both said in unison. "How?"

"But it is there now," said Stas, the King. "I recently – well, we – uh, -- well, the jewels are where they belongs."

"And besides," added Olnya, "it only works for the right woman."

"Then Anya is the right woman, because when she was wearing it, our lovemaking was beyond my wildest dreams."

"Not possible!" yelled the King. "She is gadji, not Tsyhany!"

"It is possible, Father. And it was wonderful."

"No matter. I will not allow it. No gadji blood shall taint our line! Tomorrow we begin the selection process for your mate, since you think you are ready to be mated. There will be no more discussion." And with that he exited the tent where he almost ran into Gina who had been hovering near the entrance to the tent in order to hear what was going on. She was shaking with regret. Once again she had heard that she would not be considered as the Prince's wife, and her heart was broken.

Later in that same day, the King made an announcement that Bo had left in search of a mate, but had returned because he now knew that the Hutsul tribe of Tsyhany women were by far the best in the land. He would be making his selection tomorrow night. Any woman wishing to be considered would dance for him in their finest garb around the fire for all to watch.

Gina watched Bo's face change from that of a carefree beautiful man to a tortured soul. Her heart ached with love for him. She could not bear to watch his pain. It was obvious to her that he truly loved his gadji girl. In a very difficult and loving sacrifice, she vowed she would do all she could from this day forward to make his dream of being with his love happen. It was truly a selfless act for she would do anything to make him happy, and he would never know. She would use her visions to help. A plan was forming, but in order to throw everyone off, she would dance for him at the fire with the other women.

Bo did not care about anything; he did not want another woman to replace Anya, but he did as his father wished and sat at the fire watching the women spin and twirl. They came close to him, swaying their hips in his direction, swirling their skirts, showing their ankles; then as the evening wore on, they raised them higher, while the men and women called encouraging words. They leaned forward to show off their bosoms. Some raised their arms above their heads and tapped a bubon, a type of tambourine with silken ribbons trailing below. It was a rowdy night and very sexual, arousing others in the troupe as well, but it was steeped in tradition. One particular woman, had long straight hair and coal black eyes. She had red lips painted the color of blood, and when she danced she touched her tongue to her upper lip suggestively. Her name was Marishka Davidovich. Since she was the last one to dance when it was time for Bo to announce his decision, he chose her, even though he was not the least bit interested in her. The crowd cheered, for she would make a beautiful queen and produce handsome children. But Bo had already decided we would never lay with another woman. Maybe if she remained childless, his father would free him from his position. He had forgotten about the rule of being able to take a second wife. No matter, he was dead inside, and had no desire for female companionship.

In her desire to help and in order to ease her guilt for helping the King's guards find Bo, Gina made a life-changing decision. While the crowd was busy drinking and congratulating the new couple, she slipped into the King's tent and stole the necklace once more. She had overheard the argument when Bo was talking with his parents so she now understood that the necklace only worked for a specific couple. She wanted Bo to be happy for his misery was too great to watch. She decided she would hide the necklace for a time in a hollow tree she knew of, and then once the search for it was over, she would leave the troupe and try to find Anya herself. It was an amazing act of sacrifice, because her heart still ached for Bo.

As the time for the wedding drew close, the King went to retrieve the necklace so Bo could give it to his bride, and it was then that he discovered it missing. As far as he knew the only people in the world who knew for a fact that it existed were his wife and son. He blamed Bo, saying that he must have thrown it away to avoid consummation with Marishka, but once he looked into his son's eyes, he knew Bo's denials were true. Someone else must have taken it, but no one in the camp would admit to the theft.

Gina sat very quietly one night wondering what to do next. She had the necklace but how could she accomplish her goal to make Bo happy again? When she closed her eyes and chanted over some burning herbs, she channeled a vison of a woman – it was Anya and her vision was just what she had been hoping for. She saw her on a ship with Dmytri and knew they were traveling far away from their camp. At the same time she saw a boy on the mountainside camp where Anya had tended her sheep. He was troubled and seemed to be combing the forest looking for someone. He called out a name – Anya – over and over again.

Gina slipped away the next day and took the same path she had the day she had followed Bo to spy on him. And when she came to the area where Bo used to meet Anya, she found the desperate boy and comforted him with the knowledge that Anya was alive. She said she had left the sheep behind because she had chosen to live with her Tsyhany lover. She did not go into any more details except to say that Anya was not coming back. The boy was shocked, but said that he would take the news back to Anya's family.

Bo married Marishka fourteen days after he chose his wife, but he requested two separate pallets be placed in their tent. It would be over a year before he satisfied his manly needs with his wife, and soon after, in 1866, they produced a son they named Nikita, which pleased the King very much. There was much celebration as the line of succession and the Karpenko name was secured. Less than a month after the child's birth, King Stas passed away due to a lung infection, and Bo was raised to his father's position. King Bo realized that he would never be free. He must take care of his Tsyhany family and rule all of the Boykos and all of the Hutsuls. His son Nikita grew to be a fine young man, and when he became an adult he produced a son and heir in 1892. They named him Petro. When Petro Karpenko was grown, he grew restless of the gypsy life. Too much traveling, he said. He was tired of being spit on by the gadjo and gadji. He was tired of being treated like a second-class citizen. He was intelligent and read a lot about faraway places; and since he had been hearing about America, and wanted something different for his family, he did what Bo had not had the courage to do, and he left the troupe to form a new life.

≈

The story of Anya continued and was told by Dmytri through letters sent to a gypsy fortuneteller in London. She passed on news as individual Romanis came through, but she was careful to divulge only facts to let their family know they were safe. In a way she was their post office. Her name was Gina, she worked with her great niece also named Gina who had left her troupe in the Ukraine because she could not live with the guilt of disrupting the love between a prince and his peasant girl, when through her vision she was able to tell her king where to find his son. She had brought with her the coveted ruby and diamond necklace, and she was determined to place it in the correct hands one day, but until that time came and she was sure of who she was giving it to, she would tell no one of its existence.

It was told that Anya and Dmytri eventually arrived in London, where they found themselves a small flat. They begged money for their rent and stole their food when necessary, because Anya had confessed that she was pregnant with Bo's child and needed proper nourishment. They waited and waited for Bo to find them and when messages sent through other gypsy travelers returned word that Bo had married Marishka, Anya was devastated. For a time she could not function and would not take care of herself, but Dmytri was always at her side and, finally, for her child's sake she began to eat and gain strength again. They knew it was only a matter of time before the news of Anya's pregnancy was reported to Bo, and they also knew that the new king would insist that his child be returned to him and he would want Anya to come back also and stay with him as his concubine. She did not want a life like that, but gadjo or not, this child would still carry Tsyhany blood. In order to protect the child, Anya begged Dmytri to take her to America. He agreed that it was their only option, if they were to remain safe.

A single man traveling with a pregnant, unmarried woman was unheard of, so the two got married. With papers to prove their union in hand, they purchased the tickets they needed to head to the new land. Crossing was rough and proved to be too much for Anya. She was tossed and thrown around as the ocean waves rolled the ship from side to side during a violent storm. And on one horrendous lurch, she was slammed, belly first, into some stacked trunks, causing her to lose her child. She arrived on the opposite shore married to a man she had never intended to wed and childless.

As time went on, Anya and Dmytri naturally fell into being a couple. Dmytri had always held a secret love for his best friend's lover anyway, and now, strangely enough, she was his wife. His desire to protect her and care for her turned into a passion he could not deny. When he finally got the courage to do so, he confessed his love to Anya, she replied that she, too, felt love for Dmytri. It was not the same as her love for Bo – she would never love anyone like that again – but it was a comfortable and secure union.

After their arrival in New York, they journeyed inland looking for the perfect place to live. They settled in Pennsylvania and in order to escape any discrimination against gypsies, they changed Dmytri's last name of Lysko to Woods, which was its English translation.

It wasn't long before Anya was pregnant once again, but this time with Dmytri's son. Dymtri was over the moon, and Anya was content and excited to be a mother. Late in 1871, she delivered a healthy baby boy they christened Edward Woods, which they felt was a good strong American name. Edward was the light of their life, but he had inherited his father's vagabond genes. He wanted to travel and see the world, so when he became old enough -- or so he thought -- he joined the circus, which eventually led him to London where one rainy night he stumbled on a fortune teller named Gina.

Once Gina felt the necklace, which she wore under her blouse, begin to vibrate, she knew she had somehow found a connection to Bo and Anya. She understood immediately that she had a chance to fix the cycle she had broken, so without hesitation she handed the necklace to Edward who took it back to his circus tent and to a girl he had not loved until that day. Her name was Clara, and that was the beginning of the necklace's journey through a new family line and to a new land.

Ivy and Fox – Present Day

Chapter Fourteen

She was finished. She was exhausted. Her eyes burned from reading so long. Her head ached with too much thinking and so much emotion. She would never be the same. Through the writing of her book, she could see her own marriage clearly, because due to several twists of fate, two star-crossed lovers in the 1800s in Ukraine had been the catalyst for her meeting Fox. Anya's and Bo's misery had brought about her own happiness through a long chain of events. According to her translator, the story told in the book, was a well-known gypsy fable that all young people of that region knew. It was a romantic tale of a peasant girl and a gypsy prince who had fallen in love and attempted to run away together only to be separated for all eternity. If she had properly interpreted what the story related, it was actually a true story and one that belonged to both her family and Fox's. The inscription on the cover was translated as, 'Protect what is yours. It is more precious than rubies and diamonds.' The ruby and diamond reference did not go unnoticed by Ivy and gave her chills.

Fox's mother's Karpenko line traced back to the gypsy king named Beauregard Karpenko, and another split on the tree traced to Gina, a member of that same gypsy troupe. Ivy's maternal line traced to Anastasia Pavlovich, known simply as Anya who then became Edward Woods' mother. She had married Bo's best friend Dmytri Lysko, who changed his last name to Woods. Ivy was able to find all of this later data through immigration records and citizenship papers.

It was these unusual circumstances that made Ivy's head spin. She hoped her readers would be able to follow it. If Anya had not made it to the United States with Dmytri, if their son Edward had not joined the circus, if the circus had not gone to London where

Edward would run into a woman named Gina who had possession of the magical necklace, and if Edward had not married Clara which then resulted in them settling in Michigan and producing Ivy's ancestors – Maisy and Max, and then Ruby and Sal, and the biggest *if* of all -- if Ivy had not become an author and decided to write her great-grandmother Ruby's story, she would never have known about the necklace in the first place. If Ivy had not gone to the cabin in search of it, she would never have met Fox there who was the appraiser for the sale and was just doing his job that day.

Because the Gina of old had told the gypsy King where to find Anya and Bo in Odesa and then stolen the ruby and diamond necklace, and then when she felt guilty for her betrayal, she had told and retold the story through the generations in an effort to bring back two people who were meant to complete a family line. Songs were sung and eventually the book of poetry was written until all in the region knew of the peasant girl and the gypsy prince. Apparently, each generation in Gina's line had named a girl child Gina. Or was it possible, Ivy wondered, that every Gina that had taken part in the matchmaking had been one and the same, and able to travel through time in an effort to right what she had done wrong? This was something Ivy could not solve through reading records and documents. She would be left to wonder and trust for the rest of her life.

The result was that Ivy was left with a fanciful story that most would think was fiction, but only she would know the truth, and perhaps Fox would believe it, too. But she suspected that Fox's family would think it was too far-fetched. She would explain her book as a fictional creation based on facts; it was the easiest way out.

Tomorrow she would begin the editing process, and only after she was done with that would she let her husband read it. She wondered how he would react. Ivy closed her laptop and rubbed her eyes; there was still time to get some sleep before the household woke up and began the day. She decided to take advantage of it while she could. She curled up on the couch and covered herself with an afghan and dreamed, as she had for these many past months, about a handsome gypsy prince and a beautiful shepherd girl. Her good friend, Percy the cat, curled up at her side. His gentle purring comforted her soul.

≈

"I'm finished. I can't write another word. Well, of course, I will once you read it and critique it. You know me. But for now that's it."

Fox clapped his hands together, "Great! Is it my turn now? I've been dying to get my hands on this thing. I can't wait to see what has had you so occupied."

Ivy sighed, still worried about how he would review the book. "Read with an open mind, please. On the first pass-through just enjoy and get into the moment of it. Then you can take a second look at it for spelling and grammar errors."

"Will do, captain." He gave her a mock salute. "I'm off on the job today, but as soon as I get home, I'm diving in."

"Such a good husband. I don't deserve you." She kissed him gently on the mouth. He pulled her in closer, prolonging the kiss.

"What do you say, after I have some reading time, we find some time for ourselves. Little Sal has been running us ragged lately, and with your book I haven't seen enough of you. Or," he growled in her ear, "felt enough of you."

"Fox," she giggled, "you have a one-track mind."

"Hey, I'm a healthy adult male. What do you expect?"

"Okay, okay," she squealed, pushing at his roving hands, "we'll make time. Now go before you're late." Then she patted him on the butt.

"You're cruel, woman."

When the door was closed, Ivy turned back to her son who was happily playing with his Cheerios. She cut a banana into pieces and offered that to him, also. He quickly shoved a section in his mouth, plumping out his cute little cheeks. He was so adorable. Ivy sighed. Life was good. She had never been this happy in her entire life.

≈

As soon as Fox closed the door behind him, his entire demeanor changed. He had been hiding a huge secret from Ivy for too long now, and it was weighing on him. He *had* to tell her, and soon, because it was all coming to a head now, but how could he break her bubble? She was so happy, and whatever was in that book had her totally fired up.

The day was long and tiring; he had jobs lined up back to back, and each one had its own specific problem that took more time than he had planned, so now his schedule was way off. He would have to push the last job of the day off until tomorrow, if he was to make his next appointment. He longed for the comfort of home, but he had to make one stop first and he needed to get there before the office closed.

Fox pushed open the door to Bradley and Bradley, a local law firm. "Did I make it in time?"

"Just barely," said Edith, Mark Bradley Junior's long time secretary. "Mark asked me to give you a few minutes more, or I would have been out the door."

"Sorry, Edith. Can I go right in?"

"Of course. He's waiting for you," she said in a huff.

The elderly gentleman sitting at the desk called out, "You can go now, Edith. We'll be fine." Mark Junior was the only Bradley left at the firm. His father had passed away many years ago, but the firm remained Bradley and Bradley in his honor. And now Mark Junior was nearing retirement age, or perhaps past it already, but he had no desire to quit. The law was his life.

"Thank you, Mr. Bradley. See you in the morning," called out Edith as she grabbed her purse and gave Fox a smirk.

"I'm so sorry I'm late. I was delayed on my last job."

"No problem. I know how that goes, and besides I have no one waiting for me now that Mildred has left me to meet her maker in Heaven, God bless her soul. There were so many wonderful years together, and that saint of a woman always put up with me."

"I'm praying that I have that kind of a saint, also. I'm going to need a very forgiving woman, but I'm not so sure she will stand by my side once she learns what I have to tell her."

"You'll be fine. Don't sell her short," said Mark as he lit his cigar. "Help yourself," he pointed to the cigar box on his desk. "It's after hours, and the office is in my house, so I can do what I want. Of course, Edith has a fit when she smells it in the morning. She runs around with the Lysol spray trying to cover it before the first client walks in. In my opinion, it just makes it worse. Instead of the sweet smell of a Cuban, we have the Lysol added to it defiling one of the greatest perfumes of mankind."

"No thanks, I quit smoking."

"Probably wise, but you are missing one of the delights of being male." He lit the wooden match and then waited for the sulfur to dissipate. He held it close to the cigar as he rotated it slowly until there was a glow at the tip. Continuing to hold the flame near the end, he puffed gently, making sure it burned evenly. Once he had a healthy glow at the tip, he inhaled slowly and his whole body relaxed. "There's a true art to lighting a cigar. Did you know when you turn your cigar around under the flame of the match it's called toasting the foot? I've always rather liked that phrase. It sounds comforting, especially on a cold winter night. Well, I'm digressing. You caught me at the time of day I usually begin to slow down. What can I do for you?"

"Well, actually, sir, you called me in. You said you had news."

"Of yes, of course. Here, let me get the papers in front of me." He shuffled some folders. "I'm sure Edith had it all laid out for me. Yes, yes, here they are. What would I do without that woman?" Mark opened the folder and began to refresh his memory, and within a few seconds he was back into being a fully capable attorney. "Yes, well, I have good news and bad news. Which one first?"

"I need good news, please, anything."

"Well, young man, you *are* still married – but to Piper that is."

Fox jumped up so fast that his chair almost turned over. "How in the world is that good news?"

"Because she has already signed her paperwork to divorce you. All I need is your signature, and then I can file it with the court. It will all be over tomorrow. The marriage will be dissolved, quickly and quietly."

Thinking that maybe he could avoid telling Ivy after all, he asked, "So what's the bad news?"

"You are not married to Ivy Morton. You'll need to repeat the wedding."

"What? No, that can't be. It's going to crush her. I just can't do it to her."

"You'll have to, if you want to be legal. Of course, you could continue to live together and never tell her, but trust me, my friend, secrets always get out. And when she finds out after months or years, she'll be far more upset than if you tell her now." He puffed a few times watching the glow at the tip. "I've given this advice many times over the years, and it's never failed."

Fox choked. "You mean other people have found themselves married to two women at once?"

"Not in my practice. I just mean that secrets fester, and the longer they go without being released, the worse it is. Go home and tell her. Confess and beg for forgiveness, and then the two of you can move forward and make decisions; otherwise, it will always be hanging over your head."

Fox nodded. He knew he had to do it, but it was going to be so hard. "What about the other?"

"Now that's a different story. I can't tell you how to handle that one, but tell her everything and see what she has to say. She seems to me to be a nice young lady."

"You've met my wife?"

"Only at book signings. I have both of her books, and I'm not ashamed to say I thoroughly enjoyed them. I have a bit of a romantic streak. And why not, a man can learn a lot about how to treat a woman from these books. Your wife, uh, Ivy has quite the imagination.

I've often wondered if there is a real ruby and diamond necklace out there somewhere. Wouldn't that be something?" He chuckled. "My Mildred and I would sure have enjoyed that!"

"So where are we on that," Fox cleared his throat, "other issue?"

"I'm still investigating. I have my best man working on it. He'll come up with something, don't you worry. But in the meantime, sign on the dotted line, and we'll get the divorce taken care of immediately."

Fox scribbled his signature and added the date next to it. He released a big sigh. He was so glad Piper had cooperated and already signed. At least that part of this drama was over. He hoped he never had to see her again, but he knew better. The second part of this story had yet to be resolved.

Chapter Fifteen

She was seated at the picnic table, looking out at the water. Beyond her the lake was perfectly still, reflecting the sky like a mirror, and except for an occasional ripple when a bird or insect caused some movement, it was difficult to tell where the water ended and the sky began. Her light brown hair picked up the light of the afternoon sun creating streaks of gold. She raised her hand to brush a strand away from her eyes, then reached down to smooth his son's hair, who was playing in the sand at her side. He knew without looking that her eyes would be shining with gentle looks of love; those gorgeous green cat eyes with flecks of yellow. He loved to look deeply into those eyes when she talked. He was sure she thought he was the most attentive man alive, but in reality he could not take his gaze away from the colorful patterns her irises created. She was his life; he knew that now more than ever, with the threat of losing her looming over him. No other woman could ever take her place, but what he was about to do would most likely destroy her. If it didn't, it would cause a pain so deep that he would never be able to erase it. The best he could hope for was that his story, if told properly, would explain the why and when and then maybe she could forgive him. He walked behind her and kissed her on the top of the head.

"Oh, hi hon, you're home. How was your day?" Ivy grinned with happiness at seeing him. She stood and wrapped her arms around him, taking pleasure in his warmth and his scent. He was such a beautiful man. She often wondered how she was so lucky to have him all to herself.

"It was, I guess you could say, a little upsetting."

"Really? What's the problem?" She picked her son up and they began to walk toward the house. She noticed that Fox had not even acknowledge Sal, which was rare; he must really be distracted.

"I'll tell you when we get in the house. I need a drink to relax, and then I'll relate my news to you."

Ivy raised one eyebrow. Now this was not like Fox at all, a drink before dinner? This was not his normal routine. Something must really be bothering him. Trying to change the subject, she turned the conversation to her book.

"I can't wait for you to start reading. I'm more excited about the storyline than anything else. Right now I don't care about editing and proofreading. I'm just so eager to hear your opinion of my characters and their lives."

Fox looked at her eager face, the excitement in her eyes. She almost danced with anticipation, and he knew that tonight he would not kill her joy. One more day couldn't hurt. The damage was done and had been a long time ago. "You know what? Let's not even talk about work tonight. I need to forget everything for a while. I'd like to play with Sally for a bit, and then have a nice supper."

"That's good because I have your favorite. A nice juicy roast is in the crockpot."

"I smelled it the moment we came in. My stomach is growling already."

"Well, give me a half hour and we can eat."

"Great, I'll wash up and be back in a jiffy." He was a coward he knew, but who wouldn't be. What he had to tell her would change everything.

≈

They were both curled up on the sofa, she with her glass of wine and he with a gin and tonic. He had opted for something a little stronger. Ivy knew whatever it was must be important, but she decided not to press just yet. He would tell her when he was ready.

Ivy held her computer on her lap. She was already researching her next book, but it was difficult to get Anya and Bo out of her mind. Stories of star-crossed lovers had always been an interest to her, even back when she was a teen. Who didn't love Romeo and Juliet, and what about A Rebel without a Cause? Someday she would write a story with a James Dean character in mind, dark and moody with a lot of layers to his personality. But Anya and Bo were totally different. They were just two young people from different worlds, who had fallen in love and had expected to spend their lives together forever.

Ivy glanced at Fox. When he was reading one of her new books, he did not like to be interrupted. She longed to ask where he was and what he thought so far, but she knew better. After several hours, she finally spoke. "I'm ready for bed. How about you?"

Fox waved a dismissive hand, meaning he didn't want to quit reading yet. Ivy kissed him on the forehead and went to bed, hoping that meant the book was so good that he could not quit.

Fox *was* totally absorbed in the story, but it was also a good excuse not to have a talk in the dark the way Ivy was fond of doing. Pillow talk, she said, was good for the soul. Well, not tonight. First he would read her novel, and then maybe he would be ready for what was to come.

When Ivy woke up in the morning, she discovered that she was alone in bed. She found Fox sound asleep on the couch; the manuscript had fallen off of his chest, onto the floor, and had created a messy pile next to his drink. Ivy was glad he had pulled the afghan over himself, as it was cool in the house this morning. She turned on the furnace to warm the walls; it seemed like the cooler days of autumn were coming early this year. Next she peeked in on Sal, who was already sitting up in bed, playing with some toys and talking to himself. She lifted him out and made a face. "Wow, Buddy, you are one stinky little dude. Let's get you cleaned up."

When Ivy and Sal emerged from his room, now smelling fresh as a new day, they discovered Fox in the kitchen making coffee. "Well," said Ivy, "you had a long night. I hope you were comfortable out there."

"Yeah, I was. It was fine, but Ivy, I couldn't stop reading. I read straight through." He moved toward her, reached for his son, and kissed his wife soundly. "It was amazing!"

"Really? You liked it?"

"I loved it. What an imagination you have. Where does this stuff come from?"

Ivy put Sal in his highchair while Fox poured them each a cup of coffee. He added chocolate creamer to hers just the way she liked. "Bacon and eggs?" he asked.

"Who's cooking?" she teased.

"Me, of course, you know I'm the breakfast king."

"Then yes. Two eggs, and if you add some toast, I'll be your slave for the day. So, tell me, what was your favorite part?"

"All of it. I love the gypsy line and the Ukrainian love story. I like how you used the Ukrainian connection to my family and how you worked in the ruby and diamond necklace. That was sexy." He sent a knowing smile toward her.

"Fox, here's the thing. Keep an open mind, please. This is your story -- and mine."

"What do you mean?" he asked as he popped the bread in the toaster.

"Before you start breakfast, sit for a minute. I want to explain. I need to explain. I've been wanting to get it out for so long."

"This sounds intriguing."

"Well, it really would be unbelievable, except for the fact that you and I know the real story of Ruby and Sal, and Maisy and Max, and this is more of the same."

"How so?"

"It's a little complicated, a lot actually. Here, let me get some paper and draw it out for you."

Ivy began making a family tree of sorts. "Here's what I discovered with my research, and with the help of a professional genealogist. Here's your mother, Patricia Fox, and here's her mother Kataryna Karpenko Fox, who we know as Grandma Kat. Her father, Anton Karpenko, is the son of Petro, who is the son of Nikita, who is the son of Beauregard Karpenko."

"You mean the Bo in your book, the gypsy prince?"

"Yes, one and the same, but they prefer to be called Romani or in Ukrainian it's Tsyhany. And Bo's father is Stas the King; he's your five times great-grandfather."

"So I am directly related to Bo? That's unbelievable!"

"Yes, but that's not all. I'm so excited. I've wanted to tell you for so long. Anton immigrated to the U.S. in the early 1900s – I have his immigration papers -- and after Ellis Island, he somehow worked his way to Petoskey and Walloon Lake where he met and married Yulia who is in a direct line to Gina, proving once and for all, that Gina is real – or was."

"But now I'm really confused, because Gina came to you at the Frauenthal. Those dates don't add up. She would be way too old, maybe over a hundred and fifty."

"And that's the mystery of it all. And think of it, Bo's lover Anya, and Bo's best friend, Dmytri got married, lived here in the U.S after they escaped the gypsies, and then they had a child named Edward Woods."

"But -- but that's *your* ancestor, the one who got the necklace from --

"Gina! In London! I know, right? And therefore through Dmytri, I too, can claim gypsy heritage that traces back to the same Hutsul Tsyhany troupe in Ukraine. Fox, we know the necklace is real. I was told the storyline about Ruby and Sal from Ruby herself; then we discovered the rest about Maisy and Max, and Edward and Clara; we know for a fact that the necklace was hidden in my great-grandmother's basement, and we know how it got there. And lastly, we know that once you found it, it brought us together."

Fox exhaled loudly. "Unbelievable! And the necklace only seems to work for *us*. By the way, after reading about that necklace all night, I'm ready to take it out of its hiding place. What do you think?"

Ivy laughed. He was back. Her handsome sexy husband was making advances towards her again. It felt good. "Maybe later, my gypsy prince," she teased.

223

"But don't you see? The necklace was working its way through the generations, trying to right a wrong. Gina wanted to correct her mistake in turning in Bo's whereabouts when he ran away with Anya, so she stole the necklace in the hopes of returning it to a proper heir, and in doing so she hoped she could reunite the descendants of Bo and Anya, the star-crossed lovers. The necklace was always seeking us – *us*, Fox -- you and me. We are the ones who finally brought Anya and Bo back together in spirit. The thought of it overwhelms me." She began to shed quiet tears knowing that, finally, the two who were meant to be, were together again through them.

There was silence as Fox tried to digest all of it. It seemed improbable, impossible, and ridiculous. But he knew in his heart it was true. It was destiny. It had been written in the stars. Ivy and Fox were always supposed to be together. He only prayed he was not the reason they were torn apart. He reached out, with tears in his eyes, choking back the lump in his throat, and held his wife's hand as he stroked her knuckles. Ivy took his tears as emotion from learning the true story. She had no idea his heart was breaking, and that soon hers would be, too.

Chapter Sixteen

The Marzetti family had been inside the cottage all day. The fall weather had swooped in with a vengeance, turning on a dime. One day the temperatures were warm and balmy, everyone was joking about possibly skipping winter this year, and the next thing they knew the wind was howling and the rains were pounding relentlessly. Day after day of bone-chilling dampness had been getting on everyone's nerves. Even those who didn't like winter were looking forward to a nice gentle snow.

Fox and Ivy had spent their entire Sunday keeping Sal busy. He needed a little time every day to run outside in the fresh air, but there was no possibility of that today. Fox played on the floor with him, stacking blocks into towers so they could be knocked down and piled up all over again. They played hide and seek, and they learned how to color. They played with his toy piano and sang songs, and finally after supper and a bath, the little boy was ready for a few stories and then bed.

"Whew!" said Ivy, as she kicked off her shoes and collapsed on the couch, "I didn't think bedtime was ever going to come. How many times did you have to read Goodnight Moon?"

"Six, I think. I lost count, actually. I never knew he could be such a handful. He's usually so easy going, but this weather is really getting to him. I can't wait to take him out in the snow this year. We'll be able to go sledding and throw snowballs. Maybe when he's older, I can take him ice fishing."

Ivy laughed, "Much older, but yes, that would be a nice father/son thing to do. You'll have so many moments like that in your future." Ivy bit her lip thoughtfully, then took a sip of her wine. "Fox, I've been thinking."

"Oh no, that can't be good." She punched him. It was one of their standard jokes.

"No, really, I've been thinking about our family. Things are going okay with your business, right?"

"Never better, once I pulled myself out of that small slump."

"And my book sales are picking up, too. As soon as I finish the final edit on Anya and Bo, I'll be ready to send it off to my publisher; that should be in a few days. So, I was thinking --"

"You already said that. What are you trying to say?"

"Well, maybe this isn't a good time, especially with how rambunctious Sal was tonight – but what would you think about having another child?" Fox was savoring a sip of his favorite chardonnay, when what she had said hit him. He almost choked. Ivy chuckled, "Is that such a horrible idea?"

"No, no, not at all, it's just that – well, it's just --"

"What's the problem, Fox? Didn't we talk about having at least three? I've already started to potty train Sal; I know it's early, but I don't agree with letting kids stay in diapers at a late age. If I start early and make it fun, he should be ready before another baby comes along."

"Oh, I agree. It must be difficult to have two in diapers at once. No, that's not it." Fox looked down. He could not bear to look at Ivy's beautiful face. He had put it off and put it off. It had to be done, and now, or she would never understand why he wanted to delay having a child. "Look, hon, I have something I have needed to talk to you about for a long time, and having a baby could complicate things – for right now, at least."

"What? What is it? I thought we were doing well, financially."

"We are, but --" Fox reached for her hand. He was white as a ghost, and he looked like he might be sick. Now Ivy was really frightened. She worried that he had a medical condition he had not wanted to tell her about.

"Are you okay? Tell me."

He straightened his back and looked her in the eye, knowing the moment had come and it was too late to turn back the clock. He had no choice but to go forward. "Before we have another child, we need to get married."

Ivy broke out in a spasm of giggles. "Oh, Fox, you are so dramatic. What are you talking about? Sometimes your jokes make no sense to me."

"No, really, Ivy. I have something I should have told you a long time ago. We are not legally married."

For a moment Ivy couldn't speak, as what he had just said registered. The unbelief was apparent on her face. "How can that be? I was there for the ceremony. Your whole family was. The minister said 'I now pronounce you husband and wife.' We kissed in front of everyone to seal the deal. We have a marriage certificate. What in the world are you talking about?"

She took a long look at his face, and knew this time for certain he was not joking. "Honey, I need to tell you all about it, but once I start talking I don't want to be interrupted until I'm done, or I might not be able to get it all out. Agreed?"

There was silence as she stared into her husband's tortured eyes. "Agreed," she responded softly.

"Okay, well here it goes. When I was in college, in my junior year, I met a beautiful girl named Piper Evans. She was rich and popular and when she took an interest in me, I felt special and important. I was BMOC – you know, big man on campus."

"I always knew there were others in your past. You were a grown man when we met and, as a matter of fact, engaged to someone else before we got married."

"Now, now, no interrupting."

"Sorry."

"So, back to college. Piper and I fell in love and we were physical, you know." Fox looked down and cleared his throat. He had never intended to tell stories of his past with his wife. "Anyway, Piper's father was dead set against her being with me. He had plans for her; both of her parents had expected her to marry into their Grosse Point circle of friends, but Piper was rebelling, and little did I know she was using me to do so. When Piper's dad threatened to stop her tuition unless she dropped me, it only pushed her further. She told me she would never give me up; she encouraged the sex even more and well, I was weak and in love. We were together as often as we could. One day she told me she was pregnant. Looking back on it, I now realize it was all part of her plan. She knew I would never agree to getting married while I was in college, so now she had me. I was to be a father."

Ivy gasped. "A father?"

Fox put up his hand to stop her from making further comments. "So we did what I was told to do from the time I was young. If you make a mistake with a girl, you make it right. We went to Las Vegas on her father's credit card and got married."

"Married?" Ivy choked out.

"Wait, let me finish, please. When we came back we went to her parents and announced our marriage. I knew they would be furious, but I thought by facing them like a man, I would prove to them I was worthy to be their son-in-law. But nothing moved them, not even when we told them she was pregnant. I thought at least that would soften them up. A grandchild. Who wouldn't be happy? When we refused to separate, 'Daddy' said he would cut off her money. We left in anger, but I was determined to make it work. I wasn't sure about Piper. She had been beaten down by their words and she was really upset. We went back to our new apartment, the one we had rented with Daddy's money, and she cried and ranted and cried some more. She said she had not realized how it would affect them, and she felt badly for the rebellion and agony she had caused. She didn't want to be cut off from her family, and, of course, their money. She said she didn't want to be the pauper in the family. After a few agonizing days we decided to part ways. Piper could not live without her dresses, purses, and shoes. And I could not live with a family that hated me so. It was obvious she had never really loved me. I had always been a means to an end."

"But there was a child coming."

"Yes, we agreed that I would still be in its life, but I would not take part in any Evans family gatherings, et cetera. Piper thought that might satisfy her father. We saw a divorce attorney, and then each went our separate ways. A few weeks later, Piper stopped by with signed papers, and asked me to sign. She said she would take them to the attorney the next day, and as soon as they were filed, the marriage would be dissolved. She said she was leaving college for the term and going home until the baby was born. She would be in touch and let me know where she was staying." Fox took a breath to look at Ivy. As an author he could tell she was absorbed in his story, but she was also appalled at what she had not known about him. "I called her now and then and never got an answer. I knew better than to show up at her father's house. Finally, a few months later, she called. She was crying and said she was sorry to tell me that she had lost the baby. My heart sank, but I was young and stupid, and I'm embarrassed to say that my next thought was that I was free. No wife, no child. I could get back to my life, finish college and start my career."

"Oh, Fox, I'm so sorry, but don't feel badly; I suppose, all young men think that way. A baby can feel like a trap at that point in their lives. So what's the problem, then?"

"This summer I ran into Piper at one of my appraisals."

"Really? And you didn't think to mention it?" She open her eyes wide in surprise.

"Well, you didn't know a thing about her, and it was completely over and had been for almost twenty years. I was a fool not to tell you, but worse yet, she began to come on to me."

"She what?"

"I rejected her, of course. I told her I was married and I even stopped working on the house she owned, because she kept making excuses for me to return. And then I ran into her again when we were in Petoskey."

"That couldn't have been a coincidence."

"No, I don't think it was. She had gleaned some information from a real estate agent that we were going there and she tracked me down. She was in the grocery store when I went to get diapers that day."

"Why?"

"That part was a coincidence, but she had meant to find me anyway. She said she had something important to tell me. She convinced me to get coffee with her so she could fill me in. And that's when she told me she had never filed the papers and we were still legally married." Fox watched as Ivy's face turned pale. He pulled her to him. "I'm so sorry, Ivy, I didn't know. I really didn't know."

Ivy jerked away from him, her face now a bright shade of red. "You've known since summer and you never thought to tell me? I get that she was playing you the whole time, but why didn't you come to me? I thought we told each other everything!"

"We do, but I knew this would not go over well. Look, we can fix it. I've already started. I've taken the steps to get the divorce finalized. It's over. I have legal papers to prove it. We just need to get married again, and it will all be fine."

"Fine? Fine? You just rewrote my love story. It was bad enough what I did to you, believe me, I know, and that made Sal a bastard until we finally tied the knot, or so I thought, but he's almost two years old, Fox, and his parents have never been married."

"It's not all that bad, is it? A lot of couples have a baby first, and marry later when the time is right."

"That's not how I do it. Isn't it first comes love, then comes marriage, then comes Ivy with a baby carriage?" she yelled.

"Ivy, calm down. You were the one who rearranged that jingle when you didn't tell me about Sal. I'm sorry if I added another kink to it."

Ivy was sobbing now. She began to pace the floor and hold her middle as if she was trying to comfort herself. She wasn't the first Mrs. Fox Marzetti, and it was tearing her apart. Fox let her cry. He thought it was best at this point to remain quiet. When she had spent her tears, she said quietly, now in a more decisive mood, "Okay, you're right. We both made mistakes, and I wasn't a saint before we met, either. We can make it right. We'll get married quietly, and we'll never talk about it again. No one will know, not any of your family members, and we'll never tell Sal. We'll always celebrate our anniversary with the first date. It might be difficult at first, but once we put our new marriage license in a safety deposit box, we will never look at it again. Is it a deal?"

"Really? You're going to forgive me? Yes, yes, it's a deal. Absolutely." He jumped up and spun her around. But soon the other shoe would have to be dropped, and he was afraid his happiness would be short-lived.

Chapter Seventeen

For the next several days, Ivy was cold to Fox. He understood. He had made a huge mistake by not telling her of his previous marriage. He always knew that couples should never keep secrets from each other. When he grew up the phrase 'what she doesn't know can't hurt her' was the common way of thinking. But things were different now. Couples expected to be informed of their partner's problems, especially when that problem affected them, also. He knew that now, except for one tiny thing. He still had a secret. He must tell her, of course, but he was thinking it would be better if he waited until after the legal marriage was completed. 'Was that wrong of him?' he wondered. His agony at holding it all in was beginning to show. There was a deep furrow imprinted on his forehead from the bad dreams he had been having. His sexy curl could not conceal it, and his wife had noticed. Ivy had asked him what was wrong on more than one occasion, and so far he had been able to stall her. As soon as they signed on the dotted line and made it official, he would tell her the rest.

Ivy knew her husband had not told her everything, but she could not figure out how to get it out of him without invading his privacy. She did not want to be the proverbial nagging wife. As soon as they were legally married, she would push him on the issue; but for now, she preferred to solve one problem at a time.

They had agreed to ask Nancy and Matt, their best friends, to be witnesses. They had both been present for the first wedding, and this way it would not involve family. The Marzetti clan would never know of their marriage fiasco. Ivy had insisted on hiding their second nuptials. 'It's all too embarrassing,' she said, 'and requires too much explanation.' She was glad Fox saw things that way, too. So in less than a week, the foursome went to the county courthouse in Muskegon and repeated their vows in front of a Justice of the Peace. The mood after the ceremony was anything but jubilant. Fox and Ivy thanked their friends over and over again for helping them out, then they went to Nancy's house where Nancy's mother had been babysitting. She had been told the couples wanted to spend some time alone, away from children, and being the loving grandma that she was, she jumped at the chance to take care of three rowdy little boys.

Once Fox and Ivy were back home with a new marriage certificate in hand, the mood was even more somber than before. Fox tried to joke, saying, "We're finally official. We are no longer living in sin." But that went over like a lead balloon. This time there would be no honeymoon. Hoping to lift Ivy's disposition, Fox suggested a return visit to Grandma Kat's house. "I thought maybe you would want to fill her in on some of the details of the family tree," he said hesitantly.

Ivy bit her lower lip. "That might not be a bad idea," she replied. "Of course, we can never tell her that the necklace is real, but I can show her the generational line I have discovered. She might be thrilled to know that her mother was also from the Hutsul gypsies. And I'd like to ask more questions."

"I thought the book was finished. What more can you add?"

"Oh, this is just to satisfy my own curiosity. Will you watch Sal? I need to jot down a few things before I forget."

Thrilled to see her eyes light up again, he answered, "Of course, take your time. When do you want to go?"

"As soon as possible," she called over her shoulder. She was already sitting at the computer, typing furiously and jotting notes on a tablet at her side.

After a quick call, it was decided – they would leave immediately. Grandma Kat was more than happy to see the young people again. It looked like there would be a break in the weather. Fox was hoping for some outdoor time with Sal and long walks with Ivy.

They were ready to leave in an amazingly short time. Ivy was anxious to get out of the small house where she had to keep her feelings buried. Knowing that Fox had hidden something as large as their legal marriage had really thrown her. She had lost a little respect and trust, and she didn't like that feeling. She thought if she kept busy she was sure she could get back her confidence in their love. It was not his fault, after all. Piper had been the deceiving one, but Fox had been secretive about it all, and there was something else he still wasn't telling her. She just knew it.

As soon as they were at Grandma Kat's house, all thoughts of secrets left, and Ivy's mood changed instantly. The house smelled like warm cookies and freshly baked bread. It reminded her so much of her own grandmother's house that it brought tears to her eyes. Olivia had been a mother and grandmother all rolled into one. She would never get over losing her to Alzheimer's, and then to have it so quickly followed by her great-grandmother Ruby's death had been too much to bear. But then she gave birth to Sal, and a few months later, she got back together with Fox. Looking quickly at her little family, she realized she had been a fool to hold Fox at arms' length. Family was all that was important, and it didn't matter how it was achieved, but it must be kept together at all costs. Life was too short for anything else.

Grandma Kat had prepared what she called a simple soup and sandwich lunch for them, but to Ivy it was anything but simple. The hardy homemade vegetable beef soup was made with chunky vegetables and tender beef. The sandwiches were grilled to perfection on thick homemade bread and the buttery goodness melted in her mouth.

"Grandma Kat, you are an angel. How did you know that this meal is exactly what I needed?"

"Everyone needs a little home cooking once in a while. It more than fills the stomach; it fills the soul."

"You're so right, Gram," said Fox. "Thanks for having us again. Ivy has been anxious to tell you some news about the family tree, and she has completed her new book based on those facts. I'm so proud of her." Fox's chest puffed, especially when he noticed Ivy blush with the compliment. It had been the right choice to bring her here. There was definitely some healing taking place already at Walloon Lake.

After the dishes were cleared away, Fox took over the baby duties, while Ivy and his grandmother looked over the family tree Ivy had sketched out. He heard, "Oh my," and "Really?" and "I didn't know," coming from the next room.

"So you see, this whole Karpenko line of your father's traces straight back to a gypsy king in Ukraine."

"I'm royalty?"

"Well, of sorts, I guess," laughed Ivy. "You couldn't really call the gypsies royalty, but they did have their own caste system and monarchy."

"And who are the Tyshanys and the Hutsuls again?"

"Tyshany is just a Ukrainian word for gypsy or Romani, and the Hutsuls are the actual troupe. There were a lot of gypsy troupes all over Europe and still are, I guess. The Hutsuls lived in the western part of Ukraine near the Carpathian Mountains. Here, here's a map."

"My goodness, you really have done a lot," said Kat as she studied the borders and small cities.

"And look. Your mother, Yulia, goes back to the very same gypsy troupe. She is not related to the Karpenkos that I can tell, but maybe somewhere generations back they connect through cousins or something. But the strange thing is that she came here to the very area where Anton Karpenko was living, and they married and lived on Walloon Lake."

"Yes, I knew that they had met here. As kids we thought it was funny, because my father always called her his little witch. He said she had cast a spell on him, and that's why he fell for her. He would laugh and say once he looked into her eyes, it was completely out of his control."

"Really? Well, I can certainly believe that!"

"Why?"

Ivy wondered how much she should say, and decided to go with the minimum. "Apparently, Yulia came from a long line of fortune tellers. Her mother's name was Gina, but farther back than that I'm not sure about. I do have one more question. Did your mother give any indication about where she got the book?"

"Just that her mother told her to keep it and that it was important."

"So, Gina gave it to her. Of course."

"What dear?"

"Oh, nothing. I'm still putting some pieces together. It might mean nothing. I had the book translated, and it turned out not to be child's book, after all. It's a love story, or perhaps a fairy tale, about a peasant girl and a gypsy prince, a well-known tale related in the Carpathian Mountains. I worked it into a story that's to be my next book. I'd like you to read it and give me your opinion. So far only Fox has seen it." Ivy shyly handed her the manuscript.

"Hey, I see that," called out Fox. "She's giving you the book, Gram? That's quite an honor. No one ever reads her stories but me until it's published."

"Oh, my. I can't wait. I absolutely loved the other two. I tell you what, once we have Sal down for a nap, you two go off by yourself and leave me here to read. How's that?"

Fox beamed. "It's perfect!" It was exactly what he needed -- a chance to get Ivy alone.

≈

"Are you feeling any better? You've been pretty quiet the whole trip." Fox was trying his best to make Ivy smile again. They were taking a leisurely drive around Petoskey, weaving up and down the city streets, then working their way to Little Traverse Bay. The scenery was beautiful and the small towns quaint, but Ivy was not enjoying it all as she should have. She tried to make light conversation, but somehow it came out sounding flat.

"I'm okay, I guess. I was just thinking, can you image Ernest Hemingway as a young boy, riding his bike, buying penny candy at the store, fishing with a cane pole? Sometimes we forget that our idols are real people."

"I hadn't thought about it, I guess. Hemingway hasn't really been anybody I've thought about over the years, to tell the truth. As far as reading goes, I'm more of a Jack Reacher type of guy, you know, Lee Child. Or how about Vince Flynn's Mitch Rapp series? Now that's some action."

"And yet, you read my books," said Ivy.

"Well, don't tell anyone, but I like a little romance now and then." He winked at her and her heart melted a bit. That was one thing that always got to her, and he knew it.

Ivy sighed. He certainly was a gorgeous man, but could that be enough to last a lifetime? Marriage should be based on trust, not just physical attraction. She brushed her hair back behind one ear. The golden highlights flashed and moved around her face like the Northern Lights.

Fox sighed. She sure was one gorgeous woman, but if he could not keep her trust, their physical attraction would not be enough to hold this marriage together. He had to tell her today.

"Want to stop for a bite to eat?" she asked.

"Let's sit by the water a minute. I want to talk to you, and I'd rather not be driving when I do."

Ivy studied his profile. His jaw was clenching over and over, a sure sign of stress. He reached over and squeezed her hand, and then held onto it, as he drove with only one hand on the wheel. This was it, she thought. Whatever was on his mind was about to come out. She said a silent prayer for God to give her strength to handle whatever was to come. She was sure it was not going to be good.

They stopped at a park along the bay. Fox jumped out and came around the car to open the door for her. He gave her his arm and led her to a picnic table, then kissed her lightly on the cheek. He was being so kind and considerate that it was actually scaring Ivy. Something must be seriously wrong.

Once seated there was silence as the two stared at the water. Normally, they did not require conversation to feel comfortable with each other, but this felt different. The tension was so thick it could be cut with a knife.

248

"Fox, for Pete's sake, what is it? You're scaring me."

He reached across the table and held her hands. "Do you love me?"

"You know I do."

"Trouble is this is going to take more than love. Do you want to be with me for the rest of our lives?"

"Yes, of course. I've committed to you twice, now."

"All right, then. I'll go on, but please listen without judgement if possible, and then we'll hash it out. Okay?"

"Okay." Ivy's resolve to make Fox work for her trust was lessening. She couldn't stand to watch him like this. She caught both of his hands in hers, and said softly, "Go ahead. Say it."

He looked into her beautiful green eyes, held her gaze a moment, and choked back a sob. If he was ever going to lose her, that moment would be now. "I haven't told you everything."

"You mean about Piper-what's-her-name?" she huffed.

"Piper Evans. Yes, Piper."

"Well, I was hoping that I had heard the last of her, but go ahead. Please, the suspense is killing me." She could not contain the sarcastic tone that had escaped.

"Okay, here goes. Piper had alluded to the fact that she had more to tell me other than the fact that we were still married, but I wouldn't listen to her. And when she followed me to the grocery store here in Petoskey the last time we were here, she saw the diapers I had in the checkout lane. She went a little pale, and said, 'We need to talk.'"

"Yes, and that's when she told you that the divorce had never gone through."

"That's right, but then she went on to tell me that, when she went home to her father and mother to have the baby, her father had laid down the law. His unmarried daughter would not have a child. She would not embarrass him, he said. He would not go around town introducing his illegitimate grandchild to people, and an abortion was out of the question. He wanted her to get married immediately to a son of one of his business associates. It had all been arranged."

"How can he do that? This isn't the dark ages."

"Well, of course, he couldn't force her, but he would make life difficult for her. If she didn't do it, she would no longer have an income, no help from them in any way, so no way to care for the child. And he threatened to disinherit her."

"Did her mother stand by and watch this happen? She would have been the grandmother, after all."

"At first, she said nothing, but then she put her foot down. There was a big family argument and --"

"And that's when she lost the baby?" asked Ivy, now more sympathetic than before.

"No, that's when her mother decided to send her to Europe to *have* the baby. They told her father she had a miscarriage so he would leave them alone. They said she needed time away to relax and forget."

"So, you're saying she *had* the baby?" Ivy had gotten lost in the story for a moment, but it suddenly hit her. "Oh – oh, she had the baby. Your baby. You have a child. I get it now. You're telling me that not only was I not your first wife, but Sally is not your first child." Tears filled her eyes. She couldn't control them, even though she knew she was being selfish. She had wanted to be the one who gave Fox his first baby.

Fox was in pain; he pulled his hat down over his eyes slightly so people walking by would not see his distress. Saying the words out loud to Ivy had been more difficult than he had thought. He was hurting her and he knew it, but it couldn't be helped. The silence was deafening as she processed the news. He watched her face go from disbelief, to anger, to hurt. But after a few moments, he watched as a new change came over her, and she said the most remarkable thing.

"Fox, you know my history. My father ignored me after my mother died, and now I have no contact with him, whatsoever. It hurts me to this day. Looking back on my childhood is painful because he was not in my life. If it was not for my grandmothers, I don't know how I would have turned out. If you're asking for my permission to have a relationship with your child – a son or daughter, I forgot to ask, sorry."

"A son."

"Of course, it would be." She put her hand over her mouth, trying to hold in the sob that was about to escape. "I'm sorry. I was thinking of Sal's place in all of this. For a moment I got jealous again, but I can deal with it. No child should be without his father if he is available. What do you want to do about it? Will Piper give you shared custody? Let's work this out."

"Seriously, Ivy, just like that?" Fox got up and went around to her side of the table. He wrapped her in his arms and sobbed in her neck. He was not going to lose the love of his life or access to Sal, his little Buddy. "You are the most forgiving woman I know. I will never forget this moment. I love you more than life."

Ivy held him tightly and wondered how she was going to get through what was to come. "I'm not too sure about the forgiving part, right now. But I want to do what is right. It's not the child's fault. So, where is he? How old is he? What's his name?"

At first laughter erupted from deep in his soul. The joy on his face was like a kid at Christmas, but shortly after, the light went out of his eyes as he recalled the reality. "She named him Michael, and he's 19 years old."

"Nineteen! I was thinking of a child – a little boy."

Fox smirked. "Did you forget that I'm five years older than you are? I was still 19 myself when he was born, just shy of twenty, actually."

"Yes, yes, of course. I guess, I – I had a preconceived idea. Wow, that's different, then. I won't have to be a step-mom to a teenager." A dry chuckle escaped as she tried to see some humor in the situation. "So, where is he? Does he live near Piper on the east side?"

"This is the worst part." Fox drew in a deep breath. "She didn't keep the baby. She put him up for adoption in London. I don't have a clue where he is. I don't know anything about him. For the last few years Piper's been feeling regret, and then after her father passed away, she began to search for him, but so far, she's had no luck. She said it's pretty much a dead end."

"Oh Fox, oh honey. I'm so sorry."

"It's been a real rollercoaster, and I don't know if I can ever forgive Piper. If I had known I had a child in the beginning, I would have taken full responsibility. My family would have helped out and taken him in, but she never gave me that option. And now he's out of the picture, maybe forever. And the worst is that Sal has a big brother he'll probably never meet."

Ivy frowned, a crease line appearing on her forehead, but then she went into problem-solving mode. "We won't let this drop, Fox. There must be a way. I'm good at research, and we can hire a detective or something. You must find your son!"

Fox stroked her hair, letting the golden strands fall through his fingers, and then he kissed her sweet luscious lips. He loved his wife more than he thought possible, and even in his pain and despair, his heart swelled with joy that this woman still wanted him.

"No more secrets, though, right?" Ivy said.

"No more secrets. I promise."

"Good, because we can figure this out together. I'm sure of it."

"Together forever," he added.

Chapter Eighteen

The drive back to Walloon Lake was a quiet one. Fox and Ivy held hands the entire time, trying to regain the closeness they once had. By the time they arrived at Grandma Kat's there was a noticeable difference in their demeanor. They were more at ease with each other than they had been earlier in the day. Kat had had a wonderful afternoon playing with Sal after his nap; she was glad she could help the couple have some time alone to solve whatever had been on their minds when they first arrived. She knew these ups and downs were inevitable in marriage, but why not try to help smooth them over whenever possible.

"How was your day, Grandma? Did Sal give you any trouble?"

"Why, not one bit. He's almost a perfect child. Warning: I had one of those -- perfect I mean. My first was an angel; never a bit of trouble. I couldn't understand what all the fuss was about as far as raising children goes. Then I found out the next one wasn't quite so easy. Each child comes with its own personality, and each should be treated that way. Ah, you'll find out soon enough as your family grows." Kat passed their son to his mother and noticed the quick glance between the young people. Could it be that she's already with child, she wondered.

Trying to change the subject, Ivy added, "We won't be staying too much longer, but I have a few quick questions before we go, if you don't mind."

"Sure. About the family tree again and your book?"

"What else? It's always on my mind. Working on it keeps away the dark clouds."

"Well, I don't know what kind of dark clouds you have, but let's clear those cobwebs out then. What's up?"

"Can we sit on the couch for a second? Here Fox, will you take him, please? I'm still wondering how these letters and the book came into your possession."

"I guess, the whole thing is rather strange. It goes back to Ernest Hemingway in a bizarre way."

"Ernest Hemingway? How?"

"You see, Yulia, my mother, grew up here. You know, I told you how she knew Ernest, but I'm sure there was more to it than that. He was a ladies' man, after all. It probably started when he was young. He began coming to Windemere, their cottage, right after he was born. Mother said he was very handsome, and even as a little boy he was a natural flirt. When they were old enough, he would take her out in the boat to go fishing, but I often wondered how much fishing actually got done, if you know what I mean. There's a nice little grassy spot on the other side of the lake from here. All the kids go there to 'hang out.' I'm sure they did the same back in the early 1900s. I know I did, when I was dating," she chuckled.

"Grandma, you?"

"Sure, don't all kids find a private place to neck, or spoon, or whatever they call it in their day? Anyway, when Ernest was eighteen, he left to join the army, so

Mother would have been seventeen. It was The Great War, World War 1 we call it now. I think she was quite smitten with him. He wrote her letters, and she answered them to give him a piece of home to hold onto. I'm sure she was declaring her love, but she left that part out when telling the story to me. I could see it in her face as she thought back to that time. She told me about how he mostly wrote about the cities and the country landscape, and avoided talking about war stories, which was strange because that is what he became famous for later when he was a war correspondent. Anyway he managed to make London and Paris sound so romantic. He mostly worked as an ambulance driver with The Red Cross in Italy and while carrying a wounded Italian soldier to safety, he himself was wounded with shrapnel to the leg. He was awarded The Italian Silver Medal of Bravery for that. After being injured he was sent home to heal, but when he returned from war, he was a changed man, she said. I guess they all are. He seemed to have a developed a reckless abandon and devil-may-care attitude about life. I think he was a little too worldly for her then, and it scared her. She was still young and innocent, she said, and he was too experienced for her. I often wondered how innocent she was, with Ernest Hemingway as a beau. His life changed direction after that, and they didn't see each other anymore.

A few years later, when my mother met and married my dad, they dreamed of going to Europe someday and seeing the places Ernest had told her about. I'm sure Father never thought there was anything more to Mother's relationship with Ernest than neighbors. Of course, my parents were too poor then, but later when Father's income rose, he took her to Europe for their twenty-fifth wedding anniversary. That would have been about 1957, I believe. Yes, because I was in my twenties by then. Mother told about how one day they were strolling through London in the rain and how romantic it all seemed being under the umbrella together in the old part of town with the cobblestone streets. They came across a fortune telling shop and thought it would be fun to have their palms read. The gypsy seemed startled and a bit uncomfortable when they came into her shop. She questioned them about a few things before the reading. She said her name was Gina and that she had something for them. She had been holding it for just the right person. And that's when the gypsy woman gave my parents the book. She said it was very special and was meant only for the Karpenko line. They were told to keep it in the family forever, and that someday the reason would become clear. Of course, they couldn't read a thing, but the book was so pretty that they did exactly that – kept it. The gypsy had also told my father that he came from a long line of strong men and that he would be instrumental in completing the circle. Before handing it over, she wrote some words in a flourish in her language in the front. Even though they didn't know what she was talking about, they accepted the gift and left immediately. They both agreed that the whole experience was very mysterious. Even though they asked around, they never met anyone who could translate it. They didn't have a clue what any of it meant, but it always made a good story to tell their family, and it was good for laughs at dinner parties."

"Hmmm. That place sounds familiar. Very mysterious, indeed." Ivy commented. Changing the subject, Ivy asked, "What did you think about my book, then? Did you get a chance to read any of it, or did Sal keep you busy the whole time?"

"No, I read quite a bit, and I'm very impressed with your writing style. I hated to stop, but your little guy needed some attention, so I haven't finished it yet."

"Okay, I won't say any more, then, but you can call me when you're through. I don't want to ruin the surprise, but I'm sure the reason for my questions will all become clear once you finish. It turns out that the letters are from Yulia's family in Ukraine, by the way. They must have been written by a family member. They tell about their life in the mountains. They describe flowers and scenery mostly, nothing of substance. Once in a while they mention someone's health. But one particular letter talks about the Karpenkos and a peasant girl named Anya Pavlovich."

"Isn't that the girl in your book?" asked Kat with disbelief.

"Exactly. It turns out that many years ago, your family on both sides and one line of my family were linked together. Family trees are complicated with many branches often entangling, but this one is special. There's still some work to do, but thank you so much, for letting me sort this all out. You'll never know what this has meant to Fox and me." Ivy gave her grandmother through marriage a big hug. She only wished she could tell her that the ruby necklace was real, but both Fox and she had sworn themselves to secrecy.

"You've really got me intrigued now. I will call you the minute I finish reading."

"I look forward to it. Now, we really must get Buddy, uh Sal, bundled up and start for home. It's a long ride for him. Fox, can you help me, please?" she called.

≈

"Come closer to me." Fox pulled Ivy to his side of the bed. "I know you love to snuggle, but we can't do it if you're way over there." He felt her resistance, even though she did slide a little closer. "What's wrong? Are you still mad?"

"What do you think?"

"I guess, I thought you had forgiven me."

"Forgiven? Yes. Will I forget anytime soon? No. You should know that about women by now. You've had enough experience," she said sarcastically.

"Now, Ivy. We've gone over this." Fox reached for the light and sat up in order to see Ivy's face better. He couldn't help but notice the tear streaks down her cheek. "What else can I say? What else can I do?" he asked gently. "I'm sorry."

Ivy studied his tousled hair; the curl had fallen on his forehead, giving him the rakish look that was so hard to resist. His five-o-clock shadow was getting darker by the minute; it would be thick and black by morning. He preferred to sleep without a T shirt, allowing the dark curls on his chest free reign over his pecs which were sculptured as if an artist had created him. It took all of her restraint not to reach out and stroke the errant hair into another direction in the way she so loved to do after they made love. Her hand moved forward involuntarily, but she quickly pulled it back. Tonight was not the time for loving gestures. She was still in pain, and he needed to know that.

"There's not much to do, Fox. It's done. You fell in love, made a baby, and got married. Oh, then you got married to me and forgot to tell me about the first time.

Now, you're adding the fact that you have a son – not a child, but an almost full-grown man. It's a little much to digest, don't you think?"

"Well, what do you think I've been going through? I not only just learned all of this myself, but I had to figure out how to tell you." He was getting irritated now, the tone of his voice rising in pitch. "None of this was my fault."

"Really? Really? I'd say you had a big part in it; otherwise, there would be no child to deal with." Ivy was on the verge of becoming irrational and she knew it, but she could no longer control her emotions right now than a dog could give up a bone.

Fox took a deep breath. They had not had a big fight in a very long time. He needed to diffuse the situation somehow. "Ivy be reasonable. You –

"Me, be reasonable?" she yelled.

"Yes, you. You, yourself, were pregnant with my child and never told me. Sound familiar?" He knew it was the wrong thing to say as soon as it came out of his mouth.

"Well, you should have learned your lesson and kept it in your pants!"

"That's the last straw. How could you go so low? It takes two, Ivy. I seem to recall you were there, too, ready and eager. So eager, in fact, that we didn't take the time to use a condom one time." Fox swung his legs over and began to get out of bed.

"Where are you going?" she cried, tears coursing down her face.

"Anywhere but here. We'll talk tomorrow when you make sense." He pulled on his pants, hopped into his shoes without putting on his socks, and yanked his sweatshirt over his head. After collecting his phone and his keys off the side table, grabbing his coat off the hook, he went out the door, slamming it behind him, not caring that he had startled Sal from sleep who was now screaming at the top of his lungs.

Ivy let her son cry for a few minutes as she wept into her pillow, ashamed of herself. Jealously was such an evil thing.

Chapter Nineteen

The house was dark and cold. Ivy and her son were alone. She turned up the thermostat, which was usually Fox's job first thing in the morning, but he had not come home last night, and she had no idea where he was. At first she was angry that he had not bothered to call, but now she was worried. She picked up her cell and called his phone. It went straight to voice mail. 'So,' she surmised, 'He's not talking to me.'

"Buddy, I really made Daddy angry. I don't know what to do."

"Daddy."

"Yes, that's right, my little man; how wonderful! Just perfect. You finally said daddy instead of dada and he's not here to hear it. He'll be home soon, don't worry. Daddy would never leave you." She pulled her son in close and shed silent tears into his hair.

≈

Fox ran his hand over the morning stubble on his face. He had not slept a wink. Walking out on Ivy was maybe one of the most cowardly and childish things he had ever done, but worse was not going home. He had checked into the nearby motel, and then punished her further by not answering her phone call. He would have to face her soon and try to make it right, but at this moment he wasn't ready. 'How in the world could this happen to me twice,' he wondered. 'Two women tried to hide my children from me.' Fox's faith in Ivy's love had been shattered when she had turned on him. He had done nothing wrong as far as he could see, but when he was ready he would return to the house and see if they could talk things out. She was obviously very jealous of Piper. At least he could put her mind at ease on that score. After what Piper had told him during their last meeting, where she had admitted to having his baby and giving it away without his consent, any attraction for her had been squashed like a bug.

Standing in the shower, with the hot water running over his tall frame, he began to make a plan. Like it or not, he needed to see Piper once again. There were too many facts still missing.

≈

Ivy still had not heard a word from Fox and it was nearing noon. She was frantic. Her first thought was to call her friend Nancy, but Nancy had her hands full with the twins and the remodeling on her new home. No, she would have to figure this out on her own. She decided to load Sal into the car and drive around town. Maybe she could find his car. Maybe she could convince him to listen to what she had to say. She needed to tell him she was sorry, and that she would stand behind him 100 per cent. She knew he must be hurting right now and that hurt her, too.

It was a very cold fall day, but along with the chill in the air came the clear azure sky. Many a scenic photographer had longed for a day such as this. After the cold snap overnight, the brightly colored leaves had suddenly appeared and were now reflecting into the still lake. No human on Earth could ever produce such a gorgeous view as the one Ivy woke up to every day. Ivy thanked God and her grandmother Ruby for the gift of this cottage often, but it was Fox who had purchased it from the estate and then brought her back home where she belonged. She needed to tell him how much she appreciated him, how much she loved him.

Ivy bundled up Sal, his rosy cheeks and button nose framed by his hood, just waiting for a kiss, and after placing him securely in his car seat, they left for the town of Whitehall. If he wasn't there she would cross the bridge to Montague. If she couldn't find him in either town, she wouldn't know where to go next. He might be in Muskegon, but she would never find him there. It was very possible he went home to his family in Bay City. It would be humiliating to call his sister

Kim and ask if she had seen her brother lately. Ivy couldn't bear to admit to anyone what they were going through.

After driving around for a half hour and finding no sign of his car, Ivy pulled into a small park with a playground. Thinking she might as well make the best of the day, she pulled out the stroller from the trunk and loaded Sal into it. "Want to take a walk, baby boy? Maybe Mommy can put you in a swing. How's that?." She was rewarded with a squeal of delight as soon as she uttered the word swing. Then Sal further astonished her by saying, "Ting, ting, ting," as he tried to climb out of the stroller.

"Hold on now, Buddy, we're not there yet."

The mother and child walked leisurely along the path to the playground. When they got to the park bench near the play sand area, Ivy sat down to remove her son and allow him to run free. She laughed along with him at his happiness. 'At least there is still some joy in the day,' she thought.

Shortly after, Ivy detected a movement next to her, and looked up to see an old woman dressed with a head scarf and oversized winter coat. At first glance she looked like a homeless person, and Ivy quickly looked at her son in a protective fashion. Then she admonished herself for thinking that an old homeless woman could be a threat. The woman smiled. She had kind eyes. "May I sit?" the woman asked. Ivy felt a warmth spread through her. Did she know this woman?

"Of course," she heard herself say.

Ivy jumped. Was she answering her own thought or the woman's question? The woman's eyes crinkled with glee. Ivy caught a glimpse of large hoop earrings and when the woman's coat fell open it revealed ropes of necklaces cascading over her hand embroidered blouse. Her hands were old and the veins corded, but they were covered in bejeweled rings. Ivy trembled. She did know her! Was it really the same person she had met at the Frauenthal? Was it Gina? That was impossible, wasn't it?

"Is that your son?"

"Yes, he is" laughed Ivy, "and he can be a handful." At the moment he was absorbed with something he had found in the sand.

"He is beautiful. The women will be attracted to him like moths to a flame, but there will be only one who will fill his dreams and carry on his legacy. He will have no need to search for a mate."

"Oh, my," laughed Ivy. "I'm not ready for that yet!"

"It will come soon enough. But you must beware. Protect what is yours. It is more precious than rubies and diamonds." Ivy stiffened at her words – the same words from the inscription. The hair stood up on her arms. Then the woman nodded towards the other side of the park.

Ivy's eyes followed the direction the woman had indicated. A couple stood very close together. There was no mistaking the identifiable homburg hat and dark leather jacket. He was with a very beautiful woman. She was perfectly put together, even though she was wearing jeans and a parka. Even from here Ivy could tell the skinny jeans fit perfectly, snug down the leg and clinging to her rear showing the soft curves men loved. She wore knee-high brown leather boots with heels, and the quilted parka, short at the waist, hugged her trim body like Jello to a mold. The bright yellow polyester set off the dark color of her hair. She was in a word, stunning. "Ah, so the infamous Piper," she whispered to herself.

"Yes, the viper," Ivy thought the woman said. A chill came over her.

Seeing danger, Ivy suddenly jumped up and ran toward her son to prevent him from putting a stick in his mouth. She watched the scene across the way a moment, holding her squirming boy by the hand. She couldn't tear her eyes away from Fox and Piper. Their conversation seemed serious, but there were no angry words. In fact, Ivy was surprised when Piper leaned in and kissed Fox on the cheek, then gave him a more than friendly hug, which in Ivy's opinion was held far too long for an acquaintance he had only recently reconnected with after years. Then again they did have a child together, and according to Fox they had been intimate on more than one occasion. Their bodies knew each other very well. A veil of red crossed Ivy's vision; her heart was beating so loudly that she was sure they could hear it across the playground. Should she approach or should she slink away? But her dilemma was solved when they walked away together. Piper reached out for Fox's hand, and when he did not pull away, Ivy almost passed out. Had they spent the night together? Had he run to her instead of coming home to work things out? What had she done? How could she have sent her husband straight to the arms of another woman, who also happened to be the mother of his first born son? Ivy wasn't aware of the tears running down her face and chin, which had dropped onto her jacket in little splashes, leaving water marks for all to see. She picked up Sal and ran back to the stroller, making sure to keep her back to the couple on the other side. She was no longer able to stifle her sobs.

Ivy was completely unaware that the old woman had disappeared. She was only focused on getting out of there. The last thing she wanted was to run into her husband and Piper Evans. There would be plenty of time for confrontation later.

≈

Sal was sitting on the floor playing with his toys when his father walked in. Fox had his hat in hand along with a large Manila envelope. He dipped his head slightly when he entered, hoping to delay the moment when his eyes would meet Ivy's. He slowly removed his coat, turning toward the hook by the door, when his knees were attacked by his child who was calling, "Daddy, daddy." His eyes filled with tears. This was the first time he had received such a greeting from his son. He reached down and picked up the little guy, spinning him in the air to his boy's joyful squeals. When he placed Sal on the floor again, his eyes met Ivy's. She was standing by the stove, wearing an apron, holding a wooden spoon, and looking for all the world like an ad from the 1950s. The apron strings tied at her waist emphasized her curves. She opened her mouth to say something, but there were no words.

"Hi," he said shyly. "Am I welcome home?"

"It's your house," she said coldly.

"Well, not really. It's ours, isn't it? Community property, right?"

"No such thing in Michigan. The deed's in your name."

"Yes, but – why are we talking about the house?" He could see he had a lot of work to do to get back in her good graces.

"What do you want to talk about?" Ivy paused for emphasis. "Oh, how about Piper!"

Fox's face turned red. "What – how --

"Were you with her last night? Is that where you were?" Ivy had refused to let her voice rise. She kept it even and controlled. She would not crumble.

"No, no Ivy." He stepped forward, reaching out the hand that held the papers. "That's not what happened. Not at all. I would never --"

"I saw you," she simply stated.

"What? Where? I —We --"

"Yes. Sal and I were at the park. If not for my quick thinking your son would have seen his father in another woman's arms. How dare you? How dare you leave our bed and go to her?"

"Ivy, you've got it all wrong. Please, listen. Can we sit down and talk?"

Ivy was silent for an unbearably long time, but Fox refused to be the first one to speak. He simply waited for her mind to calculate what she wanted to do next. He breathed a sigh when she finally said, "Okay, I'll listen but it had better be good."

"Thank you. Let's sit near Sal. I want to watch him play while we talk."

"No, I don't want him to pick up on our tension. I'm going to put him in his crib. Maybe he'll fall asleep or at least play quietly in there."

When Ivy returned from their son's room, she walked with a straight back to the chair opposite of where he was sitting. She had already decided there would be no touching until she was satisfied with what he had to say, if she ever would be. The thought that he couldn't come up with a plausible explanation scared her, because then she would have to figure out what to do next, but she refused to show her fear.

"Go ahead," she said stiffly. "Where were you all night, and why didn't you come home?"

Fox took a moment, hoping to form his words so they made sense. No woman had ever brought out so many emotions as Ivy Morton Marzetti had. Anger, embarrassment, humiliation, were coursing through his veins, but fear, the biggest emotion of all, the thought of losing her, was the worst. He started out tentatively, "I'm sorry I left like I did. I should not have charged out of here in a huff. I should have called. I really am sorry for that."

"Fox, I was scared to death. I didn't know if you had had an accident, or if you had left me for good. The thought of either was killing me."

"I understand, and I know it was wrong. I was just so angry that I couldn't see straight. Let me try to explain." He hesitated again, looking down at his hands which were linked at his knees. "I was embarrassed at having to tell you about Piper. I thought she was behind me, and I didn't like my past barging into our lives. I was humiliated that I had been duped by two women." He could see Ivy open her mouth in protest, so he put up a hand to stop her. "Yes, you were one of them, Ivy. You can't deny it. Piper told me she was pregnant so I would marry her, then she lied and said she lost the baby. But of course, we both know how that ended. She had the baby and gave it away without consulting me. How do you think I felt when I heard that?"

"But that's not what I did! You can't put me in the same category. We didn't have a long time affair. We barely knew each other. And besides, I didn't want you in my life after you bought my Grandma Ruby's cottage."

"Ivy, stop making excuses for yourself. Whether you wanted me in your life or not was not the issue. We had a son together and because of you I missed out on the first year of his life. You made the decision to withhold him from me. The biggest loser was Sal. And then I found out that another woman had withheld the knowledge of my son for over nineteen years. And the worst part is, I most likely will never find him."

Ivy was mortified when he said those words. Yes, she had thought them about herself, but she had always thought Fox had forgiven her. She had hurt him far more than she had thought. She hung her head, and quietly said, "I'm sorry Fox. I'm so sorry. I don't want you to think of me the same way you do Piper. I'm not a conniving person. It just seemed like the right decision at the time. I will never forgive myself for my behavior back then." She saw him soften, but could not stop herself from continuing. "But that does not explain why you would leave me and run to the arms of another woman. I will never forgive you for that."

"How could you think that of me? Really? No, Ivy, of course, I wasn't with Piper. I was alone at the motel. I called her this morning after tossing and turning all night long. I kept going over all of the details I knew and came up with nothing. I just wanted to see her again to try to get some answers."

"Well, it looked pretty cozy to me. I saw her kiss you, and then she leaned in for a long, body-to-body crushing hug. I guess, I wouldn't blame you. She looks like a very beautiful woman."

"Ivy, the kiss was on the cheek. The hug was emotional because we were talking about a son who was lost to both of us. And yes, she is beautiful; therefore, the reason I was suckered in in the first place when I was young. But that's it. She was spoiled, shallow, and self-centered and not much has changed from what I can tell, except that she truly seems to regret her decision about giving her baby away. Don't you know there's more to beauty than looks? A person's personality can kill the beauty real quick."

"But for a man that happens after he's taken the pleasures he wants." Her eyes were threatening to overflow again. She was determined to keep the tears in check.

Fox rose from his chair and went to kneel on the floor next to her. "You are the most beautiful and loving person I have ever met, honey. I don't want anyone but you. I've never wanted anyone the way I do you. We were meant for each other, as you recently discovered; our love was written in the stars. Can you forgive me for running out on you? I'll never do that again, I promise. I need you. Sal needs his parents to be together, but mostly I need you to be at my side. I can't live without you. What do you say? A fresh start?"

Ivy studied his face. The eyes, the hair, the whole package. Her heart strings were aching; her pulse was throbbing. She reached out and pushed back his curl and let her hand rest on his cheek. She remembered what the gypsy woman had told her, they were the same words that were inscribed in the Ukrainian book. 'Protect what is yours. It is more precious than rubies and diamonds.' She dropped to the floor with him and kissed him with her hands on each side of his face, letting all of her emotions play out through the joining of their lips. "Yes, a fresh start. You're mine. Mine. You belong to me, understand that? Me. No one else - - ever."

"Yes, my sweet, yes. Always and forever."

The couple slowly lowered themselves completely to the floor, the padded rug beneath them cushioning their movements. Soon soft groans and sighs escaped Ivy's lips, while under the loose floorboard in the next room, the necklace vibrated, eager to get out to perform its duties.

Chapter Twenty

"So what's next?" asked Ivy, as she poured Fox some coffee.

"I'm not sure how to go about any of this. So far all we know is the name of the hospital in London where he was born and the name of the adoption agency, but since it was a closed adoption, we may never know any more." Fox sighed. In one sense he felt complete and whole again because Ivy had forgiven him for leaving the house, and seemed to be willing to do anything necessary to help find his son. On the other hand, now that he knew he had a child out there somewhere, there would always be a hole in his heart until they could be reunited.

"Well, we do know his date of birth, and his mother's name. That might help. I'm not sure about the adoption rules in England. But I do know there are websites where you can search for babies born on a certain day without showing names of those involved. Also, I think we should hire a detective over there. Traveling wouldn't make much sense, because this might be a very long search. The British most probably have adoption databases on the Internet, the same as we do. The detective could search there, too." Ivy bit her lip, thinking of other options.

"How would a database help?"

"Well, only if the adopted child was searching for his parents. If your son has entered his name on the list, that means he is searching for his parents. We need to get your name on the list of parents searching for their children. Once you are connected, you can communicate and determine if you are the father."

"That's probably a long shot, right? He's only nineteen. Kind of young to being worrying about such things."

"Not at all. I think a lot of children wait until they're eighteen or over to look, so they can legally do it without the consent of the adopted parents."

"What if he doesn't know he's adopted?" asked Fox. "Then I guess we're up the creek without a paddle."

"That's where patience comes in, hon," she said as she passed him his toast and eggs. "This search could take years. We might be old and gray when we find him, but if I have anything to say about it, it won't be that long. Sal needs to know his brother; that is if his brother wants to know *him*. It's all up in the air."

"What's your plan?"

"I'm going to begin by contacting the agency in London. Maybe there's something they can tell us that we are not aware of at this point. Are you sure Piper is okay with me looking into it?"

"I haven't told her that you would be a part of the search. And frankly, I don't care what she thinks. But you do understand that we will have to keep in touch with her, and when or if we find something new, she has to be told."

"Yes, of course, she's the mother. She needs to know everything." The words were easy, they fell out of her mouth as smooth as butter, because the reality was that Ivy would do anything to make Fox happy. But the simple truth was that working with Piper in any kind of civilized way was going to take all of her strength. She could already tell deep within herself that Piper would be a thorn in their sides.

≈

Several months later Ivy announced that she had good news. Fox was positive she would be telling him about his son. He could barely wait to get home from work. She had insisted that what she had to say not be told over the phone. The sky was darkening early, as it did this time of year, and the air was crispy cold. Christmas was just around the corner. Snowflakes gently fell in that magical soundless way, landing one on top of the other until an accumulation turned everything a fresh linen white. The world seemed clean and polished and ready for the deep winter to come.

In the same way, Fox was eager for whatever news Ivy had. He had watched as she hunched over her computer for endless hours, searching genealogy and family sites, researching various ways to get information, but each time she came up empty, and it had been getting her down. Something today had boosted her spirits, and therefore his. They were a team now, and it felt good. He opened the door to their cottage, eager to hear what she had to say.

She was waiting for him with a kiss and a hug, dressed in a new pair of dove gray slacks and white lambswool sweater. The scoop neck of the sweater exposed the curvature of her breasts, which normally interested him immensely, but what really caught his eye was the flash of rubies and diamonds. "Mmmm. What's the occasion?" he asked as he wrapped her in his arms and pushed his body close to hers.

"Whoa, big fella. Hold on a moment. Our son is watching." Ivy nodded her head towards the play mat. But for a change, Sal was totally immersed in a new toy, and had not even raised his head when his father came in.

"Well, then, don't tempt a man." He nibbled on her neck, not able to get enough of her. He no longer cared about anything she had to tell him. He was far too aroused to think straight about anything. His hand caressed her breast through the soft sweater.

"Maybe I'd better remove this for a moment. There will be time later. Nancy is going to take Sal overnight," she said as she unhooked her necklace.

"Overnight? Why, what is going on?"

"Well, let's not stand here. Come in. Get warm. Have some coffee."

"Oh, babe, you already warmed me up." He reached for her again, but as soon as she had removed the necklace, his desire went back down to a manageable level.

"Wow, I forget how powerful that thing is." She walked the gems into their bedroom and placed them on the nightstand. It took all she had to pull herself away. "I have two things to say, well three really. First of all, I have a meeting set up with Piper."

"You want to meet her?"

"Not really. We will, all three, be there. I want her to know that I'm in on this search and that she will not deal with you on her own. There has to be ground rules. Honestly, Fox, from the tone of her voice, I can tell I can't trust her one lick."

"You're probably right, but I can trust myself. I'm just not interested. Will you believe that?"

"Yes, I do. But it's her I'm worried about. She is conniving and a liar. We'll have to be careful."

"Let's hope that she has grown up."

"Apparently not. Look at how she went after you at her house and how she tracked you down in Petoskey. She had no intention of telling you about a baby then. Anyway, she's coming to the house tomorrow."

"Okay," he said slowly. "If you're ready then so am I. So what are we going to tell her? Do you have news?"

"Yes, yes, and yes. The detective agency found out that he was adopted by an American couple. Since it was recorded that the biological parents were American, when an American couple who were living in London at the time wanted to adopt, they offered him to them." Ivy's eyes lit up with excitement.

"What does that mean? Do we know where he is?"

"Sorry, no. BUT we can assume that at some point, they moved back home. Fox, he could very well be living in the United States right now."

"That *is* good news. What's our next plan?"

Ivy moved closer, wrapped her arms around his neck, and said, "Research, plain and simple. Hours on the computer. We enter your name in every data base in this country, one state at a time."

"Then what?"

"The hard part begins. We wait. It's going to be up to him to come to us. Fox, the worst case scenario is that he doesn't know he's adopted, so don't get your hopes up too high. This could take a long, long time."

"I understand, but it's a start. Thank you, sweetheart. What else is new?"

Ivy suddenly got shy and blushed, but she quickly recovered. "Well, as soon as Nancy takes Sal we have some business to get down to."

"We do, do we? What, pray tell, are you talking about Mrs. Marzetti?" At just the mention of what Ivy was suggesting, Fox felt a stirring. He could hear the necklace buzz in the other room. He felt lightheaded and hot at the same time.

"Mr. Marzetti, how would you like to increase your family, because tonight is the night."

"Why, Mrs. Marzetti, what are you suggesting?"

"I am suggesting that you take me to bed and do what you do best." Fox laughed out loud as his male ego was stroked with her compliment, and Ivy squealed with delight when his hands began to roam over her curves.

"Nancy had better hurry," he growled. "I might not be able to wait much longer."

The knock on the door came none too soon. Fox pulled Ivy in front of him as he waited for his passion to abate.

Later that night, with the ruby necklace around Ivy's neck, creating kaleidoscope-like designs on the ceiling, the passionate sounds of two people who had been chosen to be together many years ago fulfilled their destiny.

≈

The old woman walked in the snow on the road outside of the little cottage on White Lake, her head bent low against the heavily swirling flakes. A slow smile spread across her face. She nodded, content with the knowledge that she had done her job well. A little Romani prince had been born two years ago, and his parents were living happily together creating the life that Anya and Bo were meant to do all those many generations ago. A shooting star flashed across the sky, holding its bright glow until the last second before it disappeared into the darkness. The gypsy woman's bangles jingled rhythmically on her wrist in a beat to music only she could hear. It was a melody she knew well from her village far away. The sweet tones of the balalaika and the sopilka carried across the sky, while the bubon kept the beat. She looked up toward the heavens and through the individual feathery crystals which fell gently around her, she could see a beautiful Ukrainian peasant girl and a handsome Tsyhany prince dancing under the stars, and in the stars, and around the stars. A soft breeze moved the powdery snowflakes in a swirling pattern, encompassing the old woman, and when they settled on the white carpet below, she had quietly disappeared, her task at last complete.

Ivy Morton's Family Tree

Ivy Morton – b.1981, Michigan

father, Thomas Morton --.b. 1955, Michigan

father, David Morton – b 1930, Michigan, d 2000, Michigan

mother, Olivia D'Angelo – b 1932, Michigan, d 2016, Michigan

father, Salvatore D'Angelo – b 1910, Illinois

mother, Ruby (Shaeffer) Woods, b 1915, Michigan, d 2016, Michigan

father, Max Woods, b 1895, Michigan, d 1995, Michigan,

mother, Maisy Abernathy, b 1895, Michigan, d 1922, Michigan

father to Max, Edward Woods – b 1871 , m. Clara b 1872

father to Edward, Dmytri Lysko Woods, b 1848, Ukraine

mother to Edward, Anya Pavlovich Woods, b 1849, Ukraine

Fox Marzetti's Family Tree

Fox Marzetti – b 1978, Michigan

    father – Antonio Marzetti, b.1953, Michigan

    mother -- Patricia Fox, b. 1955, Michigan

        father – Samuel Fox b, 1932

        mother – Kataryna Karpenko, b 1933, Michigan

            father – Anton Karpenko, b.1901

                father – Petro Karpenko, b.1883, Ukraine

                    father – Nikita Karpenko, b.1868, Ukraine

                        father – Beauregard (Bo) Karpenko, b. 1847, Ukraine

                          father – Stas Karpenko, b. 1823, Ukraine

                      mother to Kataryna -- Yulia Kuzik, b. 1900

                      mother to Yulia – Gina and Gina and Gina and Gina

Author's Notes

First of all, I want to thank you for being a loyal follower and reader. This series of books has been a wild ride, and if you are reading this, it means you stuck it out with me.

When I started the first book, Ruby and Sal, I had no idea where the magic would lead me. I didn't even know there was going to be magic. But something strange happened when Sal decided to give Ruby a necklace. It was meant to be a diamond necklace, that much I knew, but then it struck me that, of course, it would have to have rubies, and lots of them. I did not know myself that the necklace would hold magical aphrodisiac powers until he placed it on her neck. I actually got the shakes at the excitement of all the possibilities. Writing is strange that way, sometimes. And from then on the story took off on its own. Each book began with something new that I had not planned on.

When Gina sat down next to Ivy at the Frauenthal Theater, I had intended to write about an old woman who gave her sage advice. Again, I did not know that it would be Gina and that she would manipulate a meeting with Ivy's fourth cousin, leading to new information on the family tree. That opened up a new world of Edward and Clara and the circus, and then the story moved on to Maisy and Max in vaudeville with Buster Keaton. Imagine my own shock when I discovered that Sal, who was raised in Chicago, had received possession of the ruby necklace from Al Capone!

And as far as Ivy and Fox goes, I just intended to write about my own Ukrainian ancestral heritage (we are not gypsies – not that I know of, anyway.) Many of the names I used are in my family tree. This book took a lot more work, because I wanted to be accurate with terms and the location. I think I spent more time researching than I did writing. I pulled at my hair trying to fit the dates in correctly so that each generation would match the era. When I'm writing these involved family stories, I actually create family trees on Ancestry.com so I can keep track of my characters and where they belong and to whom. So if you stuck it out with me, I am truly grateful. I know how complicated this series has become. And strangest of all is that I thought this book would be the end, but of course, new characters have emerged that need to have their stories told. How will it happen? At this point I don't have a clue. There is just a foggy mist swirling around in my brain at the moment. But if you liked The Unforgettables Series, please wait it out with me to see what is to come, and we will discover it together. Oh, and don't forget to leave a review for each book at Amazon.com or Goodreads.com   Thank you, Jane O'

Made in the USA
Monee, IL
02 December 2020

50599351R00164